GHOST
SQUAD

GHOST SQUAD

CLARIBEL A. ORTEGA

SCHOLASTIC INC.

To my parents, Anazaria and
Pablo Ortega: Thanks for
making me so wavy.
And for my brother, Pablo Jr.:
Thanks for giving me
the gift of the fireflies.

GHOST SQUAD

CHAPTER ONE

LIGHTNING STRUCK, and a brilliant white light bloomed, illuminating the night sky outside Lucely Luna's bedroom window.

Four hours had passed since her bedtime, but the thunderstorm outside kept her wide-awake.

She'd tried every one of her abuela's tricks—including taking slow, deep breaths while focusing on the warm glow of the fireflies coming from outside her bedroom window—but nothing had worked.

Lucely hugged her knees to her chest, gazing out the window. She counted the seconds between the flash of lightning and clap of thunder, praying that it was still too far away to strike her home.

"One, two, three . . ."

BOOM!

Lucely threw the covers over her head with a shriek.

"Niña," a voice whispered.

Lucely slid the blanket slowly from her face so only her eyes were exposed. The soft glow of one of her firefly family members filled the room.

"Mamá?" Lucely asked.

Like water sparkling in the sun's rays, the firefly transformed before her. The translucent form rippled before becoming whole, solid.

Lucely's grandmother, Mamá Teresa, settled onto the bed beside her. Well, her ghost did.

"¿Qué te pasa, mi niña?" Mamá reached for Lucely's hand. Her touch was soft and warm, just like it had been when she was alive. Her voice always comforted Lucely like fuzzy socks and Dominican hot chocolate.

"I'm scared," Lucely whispered to her abuela.

Mamá brushed Lucely's curls out of her eyes and kissed her forehead before beginning to sing softly, her accent thick yet clear as the sound of rain on a metal roof.

"Duérmase, mi niña,

"Duérmase, mi amor,

"Duérmase, pedazo de mi corazón . . ."

Mamá's voice wrapped around Lucely like a wool blanket, and before the song had ended, Lucely was drifting away from the storm outside and to a place that was quiet, safe.

Lucely woke the next morning to the smell of white cheese frying in the kitchen downstairs. It was still early enough that the sun was beginning to flood the sky with warm orange and yellow hues, as if erasing the dark and stormy night before.

She stared up at the ceiling of her bedroom, which was covered with hundreds of stars. In the daytime, they just looked like beige stickers on a white ceiling, all running together into a big blob of nothing. But when night fell and the lights were off, an intricate galaxy of constellations extended to every corner of the room. It was like having her own little universe all to herself.

Lucely's father, Simon, had helped her paint the walls of her room a seafoam blue, the color of her abuela's house in the Dominican Republic. Above her desk, Lucely had a corkboard with all her certificates from school on it, a calendar where she meticulously kept track of her homework assignments, and a pamphlet for the Luna Ghost Tour. Beside the corkboard hung a periodic table poster that had all hip-hop artists on it and a portrait of the Taíno rebel Enriquillo.

Simon Luna was what Lucely liked to call an "enormous history geek." He even started his own ghost tour company in town, and people actually *paid* to hear him tell stories about the history of St. Augustine, Florida. He had insisted on hanging pictures of his favorite historical figures in every room of the house. Enriquillo wasn't the worst to get stuck with, but she would've preferred the portrait of the Mirabal sisters that was in their living room. At least it wasn't Blackbeard. Now *that* dude was scary looking.

Though it was early, Lucely could already hear noise coming from downstairs. At first, she thought it was just the sound of her dad cooking in the kitchen, but as it got louder, she realized it was . . . *oh no* . . . merengue music.

Lucely tried to pull the blanket over her head, but an invisible hand stopped her, flinging the comforter to the other side of the room.

"Que linda." Tía Milagros's voice was steeped in sarcasm as she surveyed Lucely's room. She wore the same curlers, face mask, nightgown, and slippers that she had died in. Everyone thinks dying in your sleep is the most peaceful way to go, but no one ever thinks about being stuck in their pajamas for the rest of their afterlife.

"Up, up. It's time to clean. This house is filthy! Look at this!" She pointed at a small pile of clothes near Lucely's hamper and a solitary gum wrapper in her wastebasket.

"Tía, no, it's Saturday. Don't dead people get tired?"

"Nobody can get as tired as you, sin verguenza. Imagine being so young and having so little energy! At your age, I would've already been up for three hours. Fold that colcha." Tía Milagros pointed at the quilt she'd thrown, and she walked out of the room.

Lucely snorted and put her chanclas on before going downstairs. She'd help clean up after breakfast. If it were up to Tía Milagros, she'd be cleaning from sunrise to sunset.

Plates of hot and fluffy banana pancakes were set out on the long kitchen table. Extra crispy bacon, fried cheese, salchichón, and platters of fresh fruit sat next to pitchers of freshly squeezed juice and morir soñando. The Luna family sat around the table chatting loudly and excitedly. Well . . . most of them were talking. Simon was still making pancakes at their stove with one hand and dipping rectangles of cheese in flour with the other.

"Good morning, mamá." He smiled at Lucely.

"Cion, Papi." Lucely took her place at the table and took turns greeting each of her cousins, asking for blessings from each of her older relatives before digging into her plate of food.

It made Lucely happy to know that even after you died— but only if you were good when you were alive—you still got to eat delicious food. If Lucely hadn't seen it with her own eyes, she'd think it was some sick way to keep her from mis-behaving, but for the Lunas it was all true.

Anybody looking in through the window would see only Lucely and her father, the two living beings in the Luna household. But there were a lot more of them there; they just happened to be ghosts.

"Lucely's hogging all the queso again," whined Prima Macarena. She winked at Lucely before piling cheese onto her own plate. Even though Macarena had survived a life of being asked if she could do the dance, she still loved to tease Lucely any chance she was given.

The five tías at the table shot her matching death stares. Tía Milagros reached for her chancla under the table. Lucely opened her mouth to protest just as her dad placed another mountain of freshly fried cheese on the table.

"That enough food for everyone?" he asked Lucely, and she nodded in response.

Simon smiled, but Lucely could see the small tug of pain on her father's face.

There was a time when her father could also see the family spirits in their human form. But now all he saw were fireflies. "Sometimes, when your heart is too heavy and sad," he had told her, "you lose that part of you—that connection." It hurt Lucely to imagine the kind of heartbreak her father had been going through ever since her mom left them, four years ago.

The spirits of your dead loved ones living on as fireflies, or cocuyos as they were called in the Dominican Republic— where Lucely's family was from—was supposed to be a myth, a story people told to ease the sadness of loss. But for Lucely, it was very real. When they weren't in their human forms gossiping about the neighbors or fussing over her, their firefly spirits inhabited the ancient willow tree in their backyard.

"Ta muy grande, Lucely." Tío Chicho went for Lucely's cheeks, but she ducked to avoid the painful Tío Cheek Pinch.

Unfortunately for Lucely, her uncle was just as quick and snagged the other side of her face in a death grip.

"Ouch, sheesh." Lucely rubbed her cheek as Tío Chicho's wife, Tía Tati, slapped his hand softly and scowled.

"We'll start with the bathroom downstairs, then move up to the foyer." Tía Milagros was greeted by a chorus of groans.

"Tía, can't we have at least one weekend off?" asked Manny, another one of Lucely's cousins.

"She can't help herself; cleaning is her life," said another cousin, Benny.

"But she's *dead*!" Lucely said.

The table screamed with laughter now, drowning out Tía Milagros's threats. Nobody but Lucely noticed when she made good on her promise to throw her chancla by flinging it across the room and knocking over a pitcher of guava juice.

"No ve!" Milagros smiled smugly, as if she hadn't been the one to make the mess.

"Tía Milagros?" asked Simon.

"Yeah." Lucely nodded, wiping the tears from her eyes.

"I left the cleaning stuff upstairs. Would you mind grabbing it?" Simon asked.

"Sure. Con permiso." Lucely excused herself.

As she rummaged through the hall closet in search of the cleaner that Tía Milagros insisted they use only on tile, the doorbell rang.

Who could be coming over now? The only visitors they ever had were Lucely's best friend, Syd, and her family, but they never bothered to ring the doorbell. Lucely had found Syd's grandmother, Babette, asleep on their couch with a daytime court show on TV more times than she could count.

Lucely heard a deep voice coming from downstairs but couldn't make out what they were saying. She crept down the hall, trying her best to avoid stepping on the creaky spots, and crouched down at the top of the landing to peer between the thick wooden railings. The strong smell of lemon cleaner made her scrunch her nose.

From her perch, Lucely could see that it was a man she recognized from the bank.

"I'm disappointed, Mr. Luna," the man said.

"I promise you we'll get caught up soon, Mr. Vincent. If I could just have a bit more time."

The plea in her father's voice stung. It reminded her so much of the phone calls with her mother, of how he had begged her to come home. The answer was always the same: no.

"I'm afraid the most I can do is give you until the end of October. Maybe with Halloween coming up you'll have an influx of tourists?" Mr. Vincent picked a piece of lint off his shiny jacket, and Lucely's cheeks went hot with anger. All people like Mr. Vincent cared about was money. She could tell by the way he looked at her father that he was silently judging his old shoes, faded jeans, and ten-dollar mall haircut. It was the same look the kids at school gave Lucely.

Simon scratched his head, clearly flustered. "Thanks. I'm sure we'll be able to manage."

"I do appreciate the timeliness with which you've always paid your bills, but I'm afraid with the market growing again, my only option will be to foreclose on the house."

The pressure that had been building in Lucely's stomach all but exploded, and she struggled to find her next breath. They couldn't lose their house. It was the only home Lucely had ever known. It was where her parents had brought her after she'd been born, where her dad had grown up and his parents had lived before him. It was tied to every memory of her mom, and her spirit family was anchored to the willow in their backyard. If they left, what would happen to them? Her eyes watered, and she wiped at her face.

Lucely's dad seemed to stand up a bit straighter, his voice steady. "And I would hope that our years of responsible payment would be enough to give us a little leeway now. Especially with all the work we put into the house after the last hurricane. But I guess that's not how your bank does business."

Lucely smiled. *Tell him, Dad.*

Mr. Vincent ruffled and nodded curtly. "Beginning of next month. I'll be back then. Oh, and I would very much like to see your ghost tour for myself, Mr. Luna. Perhaps a rousing performance will help me convince the bank to give you a bit more time?"

As soon as the door closed behind him, Simon's shoulders slumped, and he let out an exasperated breath. Lucely's heart lurched. She wanted to run down and hug her dad, tell him everything would be okay. But with the way he held his head in his hands, Lucely doubted there was anything she could say to make things better.

"Lucely, if you're eavesdropping up there, you better come down now."

Lucely cringed and pulled back. How did he always know?

She waited a minute, took a deep breath to settle her thumping pulse, and walked down the stairs casually. Her dad hitched an eyebrow, but she tried not to show any signs that she'd overheard his conversation. He liked to pretend everything was under control all the time, and Lucely liked to let him.

Act natural, act natural, act natural, Lucely repeated to herself silently. Simon Luna was an expert at sniffing out a fake.

"How much did you hear?"

"Huh? I was just looking for the cleaning stuff upstairs before I heard you call my name." She crossed her fingers behind her back and tried to keep the fear of what she'd just overheard—that they might lose their home—from showing on her face.

He inspected her closely, eyebrow still raised. It was like he could look into her very soul when he did that. She shifted uncomfortably, hoping he'd drop the subject. He let out another exasperated breath.

"That was Mr. Vincent, from the bank. He just stopped by to talk about how the ghost tour was doing." Lucely winced at her father's lie. "I think he might be coming to the tour tonight, so we have to make sure nothing goes wrong."

He put one hand on Lucely's shoulder and squeezed gently.

"I'm going to go clean up the kitchen before Tía Milagros has a fit. How they can make such a mess baffles me," he laughed to himself.

The moment her dad was out of sight, Lucely bolted into the small first-floor bathroom. She tried to calm her breathing and wrap her brain around what Mr. Vincent had said. They only had until the end of the month? But that was in less than two weeks! How much money did they owe? She knew they'd been in trouble with the bank before, but ever since the Cryptly's Can't Believe It Ghost Tour expanded into their town, red envelopes and urgent notices seemed to be piling up. Where would they go if they lost their home?

Lucely ran some cold water and splashed her face.

When she opened her eyes again, her cousin Macarena sat perched on the edge of the sink.

Lucely let out a small squeak before scrunching her face and throwing the hand towel right through her. "I told you to stop doing that!"

Macarena laughed so hard that she almost fell to the floor. Even though she died before Lucely was born, Macarena was like an older sister to her. Though in just a few years, *she'd* be the younger sister.

"You look pale. Mamá said you need to eat more," Macarena said softly. "Tía saw you run in here and went back to tell everyone. You know how it is; they're just worried."

Lucely arched an eyebrow. "Worried? About me?"

"Not about you. I mean, they're always worried about you, prima. But something in the air feels . . . off." Macarena looked up as if she could see through the ceiling. "And there's a . . . weird energy. That's the only way I can describe it. A really strange energy."

Lucely thought about how the storms had kept her on edge every night for the last week and knew Macarena was right.

"The others feel it too?" Lucely asked.

Macarena nodded and got up from the sink. "Especially Mamá. She hasn't been feeling well, but you didn't hear that from me."

A knock at the door startled them both, followed by her dad's voice, "Did you fall down the toilet, Luce?"

Macarena disappeared in a blink and flew through the cracked window.

Lucely opened the door. "Yes. Also, I drank a lot of guava juice at breakfast." She flashed him a mischievous smile, trying to hide the worry on her face.

She made her way back to the kitchen to sit among her spirit family. Her father had cleaned up the spilled guava juice, and everyone was helping themselves to seconds and thirds. Lucely kept pretending she was fine—that she wasn't freaking out about what she'd overheard—for her father's sake. And, okay, also to avoid interrogation by her family. But as she looked at Mamá Teresa from across the table, she saw something she hadn't noticed before.

A gasp threatened to escape her throat as she watched Mamá's human form flicker slightly, like a candle whose flame was moments from going out.

"Mamá?" Lucely asked cautiously. Mamá Teresa was the toughest person Lucely had ever known and she'd never seen her spirit do anything like this.

Her abuela looked up from the plate of fruit in front of her.

"No pasa nada, mi niña," Mamá said, smiling. "Everything is okay."

CHAPTER TWO

"WHEN WILL I GET SPOTS like yours on my hands?" Lucely softly pinched the paper-thin skin on her abuela's hand, and it sank back slowly. Once the remnants of the previous night's storm had cleared up, Mamá Teresa seemed to be back to herself. No more flickering.

"When you're old, like me, and even your butt is full of wrinkles."

They both giggled, heads huddled close together as they sat on the front porch. When Simon came jogging around the corner, Mamá Teresa smiled softly and evaporated like steam from the warm milk she used to make to help Lucely fall asleep. In her place was a firefly, dancing around Lucely's head. She imagined what it must look like if someone were to see her talking and giggling with a firefly alone on her porch, but Lucely was used to being the weird kid.

"Mamá?" he asked wistfully.

Lucely nodded.

"The tour group is already in the cemetery taking pictures of the old church. You remember our plan?"

Lucely loved helping her dad out with the Luna Ghost Tour on the weekends, because she got to play a ghost, and she'd been looking forward to it all week.

"I'm gonna hide behind the Varela mausoleum and blast 'ghost sounds' from my phone."

"Right, but not before I give the cue. Remember, it has to go perfectly this time. Mr. Vincent wasn't bluffing when he said he was coming tonight."

Simon hardly ever lost his cool, but tonight Lucely could tell he was nervous.

Her father still hadn't admitted that they were in danger of losing their home, that if Mr. Vincent *did* show up and tonight went well, they might get an extension. She may have been only twelve, but she wasn't a dummy. She just wished her dad trusted her with the truth.

"When have I ever let you down, Dad?" Lucely said. "Wait, don't answer that."

He wiped the sweat from his brow, but more dotted his dark brown skin a second later.

"It's just really important, chula."

Lucely smiled and nodded. They were a team. She looked out for him, and he looked out for her. It was how it'd been since forever. Or at least since her mother had walked out on them and never looked back.

Tonight's tour was taking place at the cemetery a short walk from their house, so when Lucely had finished getting ready, she headed out, using her phone's flashlight to avoid tripping over any gravestones.

Tucked behind the crypt of the Varela family, Lucely waited, listening for her father's voice. Despite the cool autumn breeze, sweat trickled down her forehead. Her favorite part of the tour was about to begin.

Beams of light cast long shadows from the tombstones surrounding Lucely's hiding place. As the tour group approached the mausoleum—all hushed tones and nervous laughter—Lucely cued up the spooky audio recording on her phone.

"And here, we have the crypt of the Varela family." Her father's slightly accented English resounded in the dark. *Just a few more seconds*, she told herself, *and these people are in for the scare of their lives.* Her cheeks hurt from smiling, giddy with anticipation.

"This family was quite prominent in the eighteen hundreds, but they had a dark secret . . ."

Simon stopped walking, and the group fell eerily quiet. She couldn't see her father but could imagine how he looked right now: one eyebrow hitched, his eyes open wide, his large hands held in front of him dramatically. He always knew how to sell a story. That was for sure.

"One by one, the Varela children began to fall ill and die. Except the doctors couldn't figure out what was wrong with them. It's rumored that their mother, Dolores Varela, had been poisoning them all along."

The group gasped in sync, almost as if they'd rehearsed it.

"It is also rumored"—Simon paused, walking toward the side of the crypt so he was now in full view of Lucely—"that the spirits of the children can be seen wandering this very cemetery, calling out . . ."

Lucely suppressed a giggle. Here it was.

"For their mother."

The moment the words left her father's lips, Lucely pressed play on her phone.

"Maaaammmmááááá," the voice carried through the darkness, coming from the camouflaged speakers they kept hidden throughout the cemetery. Screams erupted from some of the more superstitious, and Lucely had to stifle a laugh with her sleeve.

One of the patrons, an elderly woman who reminded Lucely of her abuela, stood near the group, completely unfazed. She turned and looked right at Lucely, who could now see her more clearly. The woman flickered, her eyes glowing a bright white. The face Lucely knew as if it were her own was now contorted with terror.

"Mamá?!" she yelped. Her grandmother materialized before her—eyes wide.

"Lucely, they're coming." Mamá's voice quivered.

She grasped Lucely's wrists with hands as cold as ice, but her abuela's hands were never cold.

"Who's coming? What's wrong, Mamá?" Lucely's breaths came in short jabs. She took a few quick steps toward her grandmother—and out from her hiding place.

"Don't forget me, niña. Stay strong!"

Lucely's phone fell to the ground and abruptly stopped the recording.

This was all wrong.

"Stop, Mamá, please!" Lucely called out.

She was now in full view of her father and the tour group. They groaned, clearly annoyed that the gag had been exposed. Lucely spotted Mr. Vincent first, who looked disappointed. Her father did not look happy.

"NOOO!" Mamá wailed in a voice so terrifying that even Lucely shrank away. Mamá held her hands up against the air, as if someone was trying to hurt her.

"Please, Mamá! Somebody help her!" Lucely screamed,

throwing rocks in the direction of the invisible threat in front of her grandmother. But Lucely was the only one who could see her.

Mamá Teresa rose above the trees around them before diving straight down and right through Lucely's body. It was painful and too cold, like being dunked into a tub full of ice.

Lucely fell to the ground, her body trembling like the aftershock of an earthquake.

From her throat came a sound, low and gurgling. *"Lucely,"* it said in her grandmother's voice. *"A darkness is approaching. You have to run."*

Muffled screams, her father's voice telling her it would be okay, his warm breath above her, the smell of cinnamon and that blue fabric softener he always used too much of.

"Papi, I'm sorry," she croaked. Then there was only darkness.

The soft glow of moonlight filtered through Lucely's bedroom window as she regained consciousness, feeling the familiar weight of her father sitting at the foot of her bed. The room twirled around her as she sat up, like she had been doing somersaults down a hill.

"Oww." Lucely held the back of her head.

"Here." Simon handed Lucely an ice pack, and she held it to the tender bump that had formed when she fell. The memories came tumbling back: the tour, Mamá, the angry patrons. What. A. Mess.

"Is Mamá . . ." Lucely started but knew her dad had no way of knowing. She looked next to her bed, but there were no fireflies in the mason jar. She would have to wait until everything stopped spinning to go out to the willow tree and ask the other ancestors.

Simon's phone rang then, and before he could even bring it up to his ear, a shrill voice erupted from the other side. He stepped into the hallway, and Lucely waited till he'd exited completely before taking a tentative step out of bed.

"Whoa." The room lurched around her, but after a few careful steps she was able to make it to her door, where she could listen to her dad's phone call.

"I apologize, miss—" Simon said, the muffled voice cutting him off. "Yes, of course. I will be refunding everyone on the tour. I do apologize about the incident during the tour. I understand it's your right to leave a review, but is that really necess—" Simon sighed. "I will have the money back to you first thing in the morning. Again, I apologize and—"

The woman hung up on him. What a bag of rats.

Lucely scrambled back into bed and pulled the covers over her legs just as her father came back into the room. Close call.

"Who was that?" she asked.

Her father sank down next to Lucely. "I had to refund tonight's tour."

Lucely knew he was trying his best to keep his voice calm, but this was a huge deal. The proceeds from one tour alone was a lot of money for the Lunas. Lucely couldn't even imagine how far back this would set them.

Simon rubbed a hand across his forehead, the bags under his eyes darker than usual. "What happened on the tour was not your fault, okay?"

But it *was* her fault. Lucely's entire body went numb as she saw the defeated look in his eyes. She would do anything to take back what had happened earlier that night.

Lucely twisted her hands, wrestling with the thought of telling her father what had happened with Mamá. She knew the story would upset him, but she couldn't keep something like this from him.

Simon listened intently as Lucely explained, and then he put his hands on her shoulders. He looked almost relieved.

"That must've been really scary for you, Luce. I'm just glad you're okay. Do you know if Mamá is all right?" he asked.

"I don't know. I hope so." Lucely's stomach sank. The last thing her dad needed was another reason to worry. She'd seen a video on YouTube once about stress being a silent killer, and she didn't want to be the reason her dad kicked the bucket.

He gave her shoulder a light squeeze as he stood, straightening the portrait of Enriquillo on the wall before retreating to his office for the night.

"Sweet dreams, Luce."

"Night, Dad."

Lucely brought her knees to her chest, fighting back tears and trying her best to ignore the headache that was coming on. She would not let Mr. Vincent take their home away from them, and she had to figure out what was happening to her fireflies. Whatever it took, she had to make this right.

CHAPTER THREE

LUCELY SAT BENEATH the willow's canopy, perching on the lowest branch like she did every morning before school. She closed her eyes, taking in a deep breath and letting the smell of the leaves and rain-soaked dirt fill her lungs. She felt the air become warmer, and without even opening her eyes, she knew the fireflies were awake and zipping around her, casting their light and comforting her like they had done so many times before. If she could keep this feeling with her throughout the day, maybe school wouldn't be so awful. The fireflies were the one thing that made her special, a secret she had never told anyone outside her family—except for Syd.

Every branch of the willow tree was adorned with mason jars of varying sizes, each giving off the amber-tinted glow of the firefly it held inside. Her tía Milagros was there, and her cousin Manny. Her grandpa, great-grandmothers—all the ghost family members she had grown up with. But Mamá's firefly sat motionless in her mason jar.

Lucely reached out for her abuela carefully, lightly touching the smooth glass before pulling away. A sob caught in her throat as she watched for any signs of movement.

Mamá's wings fluttered softly, but her light had gone out. Lucely tried to coax her awake, tried to make her show her human form, but it was no use. She had never seen anything like this happen to any of the cocuyos, and she couldn't help but cry.

She was so worried and felt so . . . helpless. If they were going to lose their house, lose the willow tree, what could she do? She was just a kid. Her heart clenched as she thought again of her mother. If they left, how would she find them? She always hoped that someday, if things got better at home, if the ghost tour picked up again, her mom would come back. Her dad didn't know it, but before each tour she said a little prayer for her mother to return. For her to walk in through the door after one of those tours, removing a scarf from her curly black hair that looked just like Lucely's, and pull her close. Lucely closed her eyes and took a deep breath. She could almost smell her mother—the coconut oil she used in her hair, the fruity smell of her favorite

ChapStick. If she were here, she'd know how to fix this mess Lucely had made.

"Lucely!" Simon's voice broke her from her trance.

She swung over and scrambled down the tree without looking.

"My goodness, look at this mess." Simon shook his head upon seeing her.

Lucely followed her father's gaze to her knee, which was now bleeding. She must have scraped it on the tree when she was climbing down.

Lucely caught a wet paper towel Simon had thrown in her direction and got cleaned up.

"You didn't feel that?"

"It's just a scrape, Dad. Chill." Lucely smiled, throwing the paper towel away as she shrugged on her backpack.

"Sometimes I think you'd keep going even if your head fell off," Simon said. "You want a ride to school? I don't have to start work for another hour."

"Nah, that's okay. I was planning to meet up with Syd to bike over." Lucely smiled before saying goodbye.

"Let's find Mr. Vincent's house after school and slash his tires." Syd Faires clenched her fists as they made their way to history class.

"How's that gonna help with my house problem?" Lucely cocked her head to the side, then lowered her voice to a whisper. "Or with the fireflies?"

"It probably won't help, but it'll feel good to exact revenge."

Lucely shook her head but was glad Syd's freak-out over the news about the house had ended. She was worried that her best friend might pop a vein or something.

"You can't leave, Lucely. You're, like, the only decent person in this stupid school. I'll be reduced to talking to the teachers for fun," Syd grumbled.

"Then we have to come up with a better plan than popping Mr. Vincent's tires. And fast."

Their history classroom was unusually quiet when they arrived and took their seats, and their teacher, Mr. Lopez, looked solemn. Lucely exchanged a confused glance with Syd.

Lucely rubbed her arms. The temperature at their school never seemed to work correctly, and if it wasn't sweltering, it was close to freezing. Their thermostat—like everything else in their school—was super old and either on the fritz or completely broken.

"Pop quiz?" whispered Lucely, and Syd scowled.

"Better not be, or I'm flipping this table."

When all her classmates were seated, Mr. Lopez walked over to the door and placed his hand against the wall. "Today we're going to talk all about . . ." Suddenly, the room fell dark as Mr. Lopez flipped off the light switch and continued, "Witches!" The class erupted into squeals and giggles.

The darkness soon softened as the sunlight from the adjacent playground spilled through the windows. A chill ran down Lucely's spine as she waited excitedly for the lesson to begin. She could practically feel Syd bouncing in her seat. Syd was obsessed with anything even remotely supernatural or scary. Especially witches.

Mr. Lopez wrote the words *Las Brujas Moradas* with an elegant flourish on the chalkboard and turned around to face the classroom, his eyebrows knit.

"Who knows who Las Brujas Moradas were?"

Before he had even finished the sentence, Syd's hand waved frantically in the air.

Mr. Lopez pointed at Syd and smiled.

Syd cleared her throat and stood up. She threw her long black braids over her shoulders, ignoring the side-eye from some of her classmates. How she managed to be so cool and dorky at the same time would always be a mystery to Lucely. "It's just confidence," Syd would always say, mimicking the same calm as her brass-band musician dad or drummer mom. Lucely hoped if she spent enough time with her best friend, one day some of that would rub off on her.

"The legend goes that Las Brujas Moradas were a coven of witches from Spain who fled to St. Augustine during the Spanish Inquisition. They chose the name Moradas because purple is believed to be a powerful color connected to mysticism and the supernatural. It's said you can—"

Mr. Lopez held his hand up. "No need for a full history lesson just yet, Syd, but you'll get your chance. Thank you."

Syd slid back into her chair with a look of disappointment on her face. She lived for anything having to do with magic and could talk about it for hours. It was her absolute favorite thing, after macaroni-and-cheese pizza.

"Syd is exactly right. The witches of the Purple Coven, as they are called in English, were powerful and feared, dangerous and cunning. There is a legend that says a secret book of spells that belonged to the Purple Coven was lost long ago. That it was buried somewhere secret. Somewhere dangerous."

"Do you know where it might have been buried?" Syd blurted out before raising her hand.

"Nobody knows for sure. If the legend is true, and anything was hidden, it likely would've been found by now."

Syd scrunched her nose, and Lucely held in a laugh. That was not the answer she was hoping for.

"What kinds of things are in the book?" asked another one of her classmates.

"Love spells," Mr. Lopez began.

The class laughed in unison, and some kids made retching noises.

"Settle down. There were also spells for good luck, fortune, and even"—Mr. Lopez raised one eyebrow ominously—"a spell to raise the dead. To bring them back from the underworld, as ghosts."

"Ghosts aren't real," one of her classmates said.

"Raise your hand," Mr. Lopez responded. "And yes, many people think so, but others think they walk among us. Maybe even here in this very classroom."

The class was silent. Lucely shivered in her seat, an eerie feeling washing over her. Ghosts might be a joke to her classmates, but she knew better. She knew the ghost world was a lot closer than anyone thought.

"Some say that the Purple Coven even had spells that would make those ghosts visible to us, to make the dead that walk the earth as real as you and me. No one knows what eventually became of them, but rumor has it their spirits still roam the streets of St. Augustine, seeking revenge for being driven from their homes. But those are just silly urban legends . . . Or are they?"

Lucely fumbled with her combination lock, trying for the third time to get her locker open.

"Helloooo . . . Lucelyyyy . . . Where *are* you today?" Syd waved her hand in front of Lucely's face. The smell of her bubble-gum lip gloss permeated the air.

"Huh? Sorry, I have a lot on my mind."

"I was thinking about what you told me." Syd lowered her voice. "About the thing with your fireflies. What if we found that book Mr. Lopez was talking about? The one with the ghost spell."

Lucely raised an eyebrow. "Mr. Lopez said it was just an urban legend."

"That's what teachers always say, and then after school they put on their dad jeans and go searching for things themselves. Lucely, if we found that book, don't you think it could help Mamá?"

"How?" Lucely was skeptical, but she knew better than to underestimate Syd. She was always good at coming up with a plan.

"Think about it! If the spell is able to *wake the dead*, it could wake Mamá, right?"

Lucely scratched her chin. She knew more than anyone that ghosts were real and that other people wanted them to be too. It's why they spent money to be freaked out on tours.

And if there was a spell to wake them, maybe that's exactly what they needed to help Mamá.

"I admit, it's the best plan I've heard yet," Lucely conceded. There might be nothing she could do about losing her home, but she could at least try to save her firefly family.

"Technically, it's the only plan you've heard yet." Syd laughed.

"I'm sorry I'm being so negative. I'm just worried about Mamá and the whole house thing."

"Duh. That's why I'm trying to help you! Mr. Vincent said your dad had until the end of the month to come up with the rent money, right? Well, that should be plenty of time to save the fireflies and help your dad's ghost tour stop sucking. We should marathon every season of *Phantom Hunters* for ideas and come up with a plan. Leave it to me."

Phantom Hunters was Syd's favorite TV show, where three women and a cameraman search for paranormal activity in abandoned hospitals and other haunted locales.

"Dad's tour does not suck!"

Syd cocked her head to the side. A knowing look on her face.

"Okay, maybe it sucks a little, but be less harsh, Syd. Sheesh. I'm delicate and a Hufflepuff." Lucely bit her lip. "I mean, it might work, sure. But I dunno. If the book were real, someone would've found it a long time ago."

"Exactly. And if anyone found that book, I bet you I know who it was."

A smile spread across Syd's face, her eyes meeting Lucely's. They were clearly thinking the same thing, because a moment later they answered at the exact same time.

"Babette."

CHAPTER FOUR

ORANGE-AND-YELLOW FLOWERS DOTTED
the ivy that hung from the balconies above Lucely and Syd as
they rode their bikes through town. When it came to
Halloween, every store on San Marco Avenue went all out
with their decorations. Fake tombstones lined the sidewalks
with names like Emma Goner and Ricky D. Bones. The candy
store was decorated like a gingerbread house, and one of the
workers stood at the door dressed as a witch, inviting children
inside. There were cobwebs and fake spiders on everything
from the lampposts to the mailboxes, and green and orange
lights adorned the trees, which looked even cooler and spook-
ier at night.

It was a crisp day, the kind where you could get away

with shorts but still needed a sweater. Their baseball caps were pulled low to shield from the sun. Syd's cap had a macaroni noodle on it, and Lucely's a hunk of cheese—Babette's weird Christmas gifts to them last year.

Syd's grandmother, Babette, lived on the north side of town, just a few miles from school in an old house in which she also ran her occult shop, Babette's Baubles.

A small, hand-painted sign just off the side of the main road marked the gravelly inlet where Babette's customers could park their cars. From there, visitors had to walk along a narrow dirt path surrounded by a dense cover of trees until they reached the clearing where Babette's house stood. Finally, they could either take a rickety footbridge over the swampy, alligator-infested water or paddle across using the small rowboat that Babette kept moored to a dock just out of sight. If you didn't know to search for it, you'd never know it was there. The shop was attached to Babette's house, hints of purple peeking out of the few spots where the ivy hadn't completely obscured the paint.

Lucely and Syd stood in the clearing weighing their options: the footbridge or the rowboat. Even though Lucely knew that the footbridge was only enchanted to look old and decrepit, she still couldn't help but feel as if it might collapse underneath them at any moment.

The girls piled their bikes into the small wooden boat—careful to balance the weight so they wouldn't capsize—and paddled the short distance across the water.

The house seemed to sway in response to the wind, making sounds like an ancient owl. Wisteria adorned every window, and although it looked lovely, Lucely knew that wasps frequented the plants outside Babette's home, and she seemed to like them there.

They parked their bikes on the porch before going inside.

The shop smelled of incense and fresh bread. Babette loved to bake, and there was always something in the oven.

The door opened with a low, rumbling creak, as if saying, "Come iiiiiin."

The moment they stepped inside, the cats descended on them.

Each of Babette's eight cats was named after a *Goonies* character, thanks to Syd. Mouth, a scraggly mange of a cat, began wailing incessantly, looking for either attention or a snack. Sloth, a brawny sphinx who was missing an ear after getting into a fight with another cat, rolled around on top of a table in the entryway, knocking over a few cobwebbed candelabras. But it was Chunk who rubbed her hefty body against Lucely's leg and let out a low, clipped "meow" before rolling onto her back to display her massive furry belly.

"Hey, Chunk," Lucely cooed as she bent down to give her what she wanted: tummy rubs.

Lucely had been here before but usually only for sleepovers with Syd, never for anything like this. Babette's house was just one of those places with never-ending secrets, a labyrinth of passageways and hidden rooms to explore. She imagined it would fit better in Diagon Alley than in the Florida swamp. There were doors Lucely had never even opened—doors you thought led one place but took you into a completely different part of the house. It could be frustrating when you needed the bathroom in the middle of the night.

The wing of the house where Babette conducted her business was just off the main entryway, leading to a small hut with plants, onions, and knickknacks hanging from the ceiling. It looked small, but when you went inside, the shop was much bigger than it appeared. The walls were lined with candles (some lit), books (some turning pages of their own accord), and all sorts of strange items. Potions for everything from bad luck to baldness sat on tables and shelves throughout the store. And everywhere you looked, there seemed to be a cat tail swaying or little paws sticking out from cozy corners.

"Close the door, you two! Or else you're gonna let one of the cats out." A raspy but strong voice came from the back room. Syd jumped at the sound of her grandmother's voice, and Lucely quickly closed the door.

"How did she even know it was us?" Lucely whispered.

"Witch, remember?" Syd mouthed, the corner of her lip curling up.

There was a long-standing rumor in town that Babette was more than just some reclusive peddler of rare oddities and objects of the occult—that she was *actually* a witch. Syd seemed more pleased than bothered by the rumor. She threatened to hex anyone who dared make fun of her beloved Babette, and they eventually got either too bored or too scared to keep bullying her.

"Why aren't you girls in school?" Babette appeared from the back room, her beautiful gray dreadlocks piled high on her head. She swept through the room as if she were floating, like her feet were not even touching the ground. Tall and elegant, with high cheekbones and warm, dark skin the same color as Syd's, she wore a thin, blue caftan with long sleeves and silk trim.

"It's four in the afternoon, Nana. Did you just wake up?" Syd hugged her grandmother.

"When you get to be my age, girly, no one can tell you *when* or *for how long* you get to sleep." Babette let out an amused laugh.

"Oh, baby." She took Lucely's chin in her hands. "You're getting so *big*."

"Hello, Babette." Lucely's cheeks burned.

She was used to her dad being affectionate with her, but Syd's family took it to a whole new level.

"Are you just here to pet the cats or what?" Babette hitched an eyebrow at Lucely, who had picked up Chunk and was cradling her like a baby. Chunk wasn't the cuddliest cat, but she didn't mind being carried. Any excuse to not walk was fine by her.

"Can't we just pop by for a visit without having some ulterior motive?" Syd said, feigning offense.

Babette pursed her lips. She was always suspicious. "You can look around but be *careful*. Don't you go breaking anything otherwise I'll make you dust the bookcases until you're as old as I am."

"Meow," Chunk added.

Both girls groaned.

Babette had about thirty large bookcases filled with scrolls and books in varied sizes that looked as if dust had been gathering on them since the printing press was invented. Once, they had made the mistake of coming over to her shop and making too much noise as she helped customers and got roped into helping her dust them. It had taken them hours to finish, and after about the seven-hundredth sneeze, Lucely vowed never to dust again.

But it had been the day Lucely and Syd came over to do research for a class project that something curious happened. They had been going through Babette's collection of local lore and history books when Lucely had accidentally revealed a door hidden within the folds of the room. They had barely gotten a chance to peek into the secret room before Babette found them. Her face ashen, eyes wide.

"That section is forbidden," Babette had said, dragging them out of the room. "Bad things come to little girls who meddle."

She had made them promise not to go looking for it again, so she *must* have been hiding something in there.

Babette went into the kitchen to make her tea for "the headache you two will most likely give me" while Lucely and Syd walked toward the bookshelves at the back of the shop. Chunk and Mikey, the smallest of all the cats, followed on their heels.

The girls searched the highest shelves first, using a teetering stack of books to boost them up.

"Do you at least remember what the book-key thing looked like?" Syd asked.

Lucely bit her lip. "Umm . . . not really. It was old, and it had a dark cover."

"Oh great, may as well be camouflaged then."

The silence stretched between them as they tested each book. It was like trying to find the needle in a haystack. Chunk was stretched out on a pile of books, already snoring. How cats could fall asleep in such weird places, Lucely would never understand.

Syd broke the silence. "I don't want to jinx anything . . . but if you and your dad had to move, where would you go?"

Lucely didn't want to think about it. But she had anyway, even if she couldn't admit it.

"Not sure. Somewhere boring I bet."

"I won't be there, so, duh."

"If we have to leave . . ." Lucely started, a knot forming in her throat. She shifted a few more books around before stealing a quick glance at Syd, embarrassment washing over her. She knew Syd wouldn't push it, but she didn't have anyone else to talk to about it, so she continued, "If we move, I'm afraid that we're gonna lose our connection with the fireflies."

Syd pulled her in for a hug. "Don't you worry about that. We'll just make sure you don't have to move. We can chain ourselves to the tree! Or have a massive bake sale fund-raiser and invite the whole town! You're not in this alone."

Lucely smiled to hide the way her heart tugged painfully. But Syd was right; she wasn't alone. Her mom might not be around anymore, but her dad was always there when Lucely needed him most. And Syd could be pushy, but she was also always there when it counted most with the words Lucely needed to hear. This was why they were best friends.

"Let's try some of the higher shelves," Syd said, rolling the sliding wooden ladder from the corner of the room to the nearest bookcase. Lucely kept looking over her shoulder, worried about Babette finding them snooping.

"If she comes in, we can just say we're doing research for a school project again, no biggie." Syd shrugged, stepping onto the ladder.

Lucely slowly pushed the ladder as Syd tried the rest of the musty books without success.

"Well, that was an epic waste of time," Lucely huffed, leaning back against the bookcase she had just finished searching. Before she even realized what was happening, Lucely found herself falling backward through the air. The hardwood floor greeted her with a *thud*.

Syd spun at the commotion to see Lucely in a daze as she tried to reorient herself.

"Luce!" Syd rushed to her side. "Are you okay?"

"What happened?" Lucely's vision slowly came back into focus. She turned toward the wall of the room. Where the bookcase had been just moments before now stood the entrance to Babette's secret room.

Syd pulled out her phone and turned on the flashlight to illuminate the room as they cautiously inched inside. A small collection of books sat tucked away on a low shelf with a label that read: DO NOT TOUCH. Just below, in a fine script, it said, AND THAT MEANS YOU, SYDNEY FAIRES!

"Your grandma is so freaky sometimes."

"Says the girl who lives with ghosts," Syd said.

"You got me there." Lucely grabbed one of the books and opened it, causing a cloud of dust to erupt in her face. A fit of coughs clawed at her throat as she strained to hold them back, afraid of alerting Babette.

Syd was helping Lucely wipe the dust off her face when Lucely noticed the corner of what looked like a crudely bound notebook under a pile of tattered papers. She fished the book out.

"What is it?" Syd asked. It appeared to be bound in some sort of short brown fur and looked like it would fall apart at any moment.

Lucely flipped through to a random page. The words *For the Removal of Stubborn Warts* were scribbled at the top followed by instructions in a language she couldn't read and a list of ingredients.

"Could this be . . ." Lucely started.

"A book of magic?" Syd and Lucely said in unison.

Every page was filled with scrawled handwriting: spells

to reverse wrinkles, to recover a lost item, to give an enemy the stomach flu. Lucely turned back to the first page to see if there were any clues about whom the book belonged to. "There's a list of names here, but they're all crossed out except for the last one: Anastasia M."

"Never heard of her," Syd said.

They scanned through every page in search of anything that might help revive Mamá and stop whatever was hurting Lucely's fireflies. As she came to the last few pages, her hope dimmed.

"Wait!" Lucely gasped. "A few pages are missing—torn out by the looks of it."

"Maybe the spell we need *was* here." Syd examined the section with the torn-out pages.

Just then, Chunk mewed and Babette's voice carried into the room from the kitchen. "You girls want any snacks? I've got some leftover frog leg stew and some chicken livers that I can fry up if you're hungry."

Lucely's stomach plunged like she was going down a steep roller coaster.

"Let's get out of here," Lucely whispered, stuffing the spell book into the waistband of her jeans before scrambling out of the room. Together they worked to get the bookcase closed.

"If she catches us, we'll be stuck doing her chores until

we're old and wrinkly, like, twenty-seven!" Syd whispered frantically as they tried to close the heavy secret entrance. Just as the bookcase settled back into place, Babette walked into the room.

Lucely's heart was pounding. She was sure Babette could see the fear in her eyes just as sure as Lucely could see the sweat on Syd's brow.

"What are you girls up to? Lookin' more scared than two trapped mice." Babette hitched an eyebrow.

"We were just looking around and Lucely read a story about a witch with no eyes and got freaked out and . . ." Syd babbled nervously.

At the same moment, Lucely blurted out, "We were looking for a book about Las Brujas Moradas for a school project. We learned about them in class today."

Syd narrowed her eyes at Lucely, her mouth still open, unable to respond.

Babette pursed her lips. "Out, out. This room is full of all sorts of things you two have no business involving yourselves with or knowing about."

The girls cringed as Babette ushered them out.

"Wait just one minute," Babette said.

Lucely and Syd froze. The spell book tucked under Lucely's shirt seemed to be getting hot against her skin. They'd been caught, for sure.

"Stay put." Babette pointed a finger at them before disappearing back into the library.

"Oh my gosh. She's going to lock us up in her basement and never let us out," Syd squealed.

"It was nice knowing you, Syd. I'll miss you when we're both dead."

Syd winced just as Babette came back into the room, cradling something in her arms.

"I do have one book you might like." Babette still looked angry, but there was a mischievous twinkle in her eye. "*Magic and the Occult: A History.*"

Both girls looked at each other.

Babette sighed as she handed it over to Lucely. "This book has everything you'd want to know about witches, including the greatest coven there ever was: Las Brujas Moradas."

Lucely held in a gasp.

"I thought they were supposed to be evil," Syd said.

"Bah! Don't believe everything your teachers recite from their history books. Everyone wants to paint a powerful woman out to be wicked. How do you think witches got their name in the first place, hmm?"

The book didn't just look old; it looked like it could spontaneously turn into ashes in her arms. And it had what looked like squished mouse poop on the inside of the cover.

"Where did you find this, Babette?" Lucely tried her best not to look too grossed out.

Babette paused. "In one of the local cemeteries, I think."

"In a cemetery? What kind of place is that for a book?" Syd asked.

"What better place to bury the truth than with the dead?"

"That was close." Lucely put her helmet on over her massive curls and got on her bike.

"I felt like I was going to barf, I was so scared," Syd said.

"Me too." Lucely shook her head. "So, what time do you think we should go?"

Syd looked confused. "Go where?"

"Do you know who Anna McMaster is?"

Syd shook her head no.

"There's a mausoleum in the cemetery next to my house that belonged to the McMasters family," Lucely said. "They had a daughter named Anna who ran away when she was seventeen—"

"Do you think she could be the Anastasia we're looking for?" Syd cut in.

Lucely hitched an eyebrow at Syd with an expression that meant *you gonna let me finish?* Lucely continued, "Years passed with no word from her, so Anna's parents thought she had died and decided to bury a casket with some of her belongings. Maybe the missing pages were buried with her."

"Are you suggesting we go and dig up someone's grave?!" Syd looked like she was about to pass out. "How the heck do you know all that anyways?"

Lucely laughed. "From helping out my dad with the ghost tour, duh! And there's only one way to find out. I saw a ring of skeleton keys near where we found the book; maybe one of those will unlock the mausoleum. We'll have to sneak back in later tonight when Babette is asleep to retrieve them."

"Deal! I like this reckless side of you, Lucely. I just wish it didn't have to be because of the whole being-kicked-out-of-your-house thing."

"I know, me neither. Who knows, maybe something good will come out of it," Lucely said, but as she peddled away from Babette's, her stomach sank. Something told her this was only the beginning of their problems.

CHAPTER FIVE

IN THE PAST HOUR, Lucely had eaten three Oreos, one pickle, a few crackers, and a handful of old candy she definitely should not have had. And she was still hungry.

Since her dad was always working on the tour or walking around town handing out flyers to drum up business, Lucely had recently been promoted to unsupervised stove use, and a grilled cheese sandwich sounded perfect right about now.

Guilt gnawed at Lucely as she melted butter in the cast iron pan. Through the kitchen window, she could see faint twinkling within the willow's branches.

"The key to grilled cheese is to use as much butter as possible," a familiar voice said from behind her.

Lucely jumped. "I told you not to sneak up on me like that, Manny! And I already put, like, a whole stick of butter in."

"You need two, *minimum*." Manny smiled, hopping up to sit on the counter next to Lucely to supervise.

Manny was fifteen—or at least he had been ten years ago, before the accident. He would've been an adult now, probably with a job and maybe even kids of his own. Instead he looked much the same as he did in all the pictures they had of him. His dark hair was cropped close to his scalp, and his fresh, barbershop-shaved part curved to the right. A small, gold hoop earring gleamed from one ear, and his deep dimples showed whenever he smiled. Now he was just a tiny bit see-through.

"Hey, Manny, do you have any idea what happened to Mamá?" Lucely flipped her sandwich in the pan, the smell of browning butter filling the air.

Her cousin shrugged. "Dunno. I thought she was just asleep at first, but it's weird . . . Ever since last night, I haven't been able to feel her spirit energy."

Lucely's heart dropped, and she turned to him. "I hope she's okay."

"I'm sure she is." Manny smiled. "She's old, even for a spirit, but she's strong. I'll bet she's just taking one of Babette's power naps." Some of the spirit family knew her from their living years and some from her visits to Lucely's house, but they all knew about Babette.

Lucely's face softened, a smile reaching her lips. But as she sat down to eat her sandwich, she noticed something was off with Manny. He looked normal, for a ghost. But he looked scared.

"You okay, Manny?"

He sat at the table opposite Lucely and looked down. "It all feels wrong, prima. For as long as I've been here, living like this, I've had moments of sadness for my old life. But for the most part, I've been happy. Happy to be around family and still be able to talk and joke and do stuff. Lately though, I'm starting to forget things. Things about when I was alive. And what that felt like." He looked up, and his eyes were watering. And something else. They were red.

Lucely's heart thumped hard, her breathing jagged. A puff of mist came out from her mouth, and she suddenly realized how cold it had become. She looked down, and her grilled cheese sandwich had sprouted tiny icicles along the edges.

"What's going on?"

"I don't know." Manny's body began to levitate. Just like Mamá's had in the cemetery.

The table started to shake, gently at first and then building to a rattle like there was an earthquake in their kitchen. Lucely was up and on the other side of the room as quickly as she could manage while keeping her eyes on Manny.

"Manny! Please, come down." She didn't know what else to say or do. She was scared for her cousin. Scared for herself.

"Something bad is coming." Manny's eyes opened wide. "It's coming with the rain."

"What are you talking about? What's coming?" Lucely wanted to run to her room and hide under the covers. Instead, she stood her ground and kept her eyes on her cousin. She tried to slow her breathing and stay calm, but she could almost smell the twisted iron and burnt rubber wafting around her cousin, like a strange and deadly aura.

"Manny, you're safe. I'm here. Please come down." Lucely reached up once more and this time, Manny reached back. His fingers looked cold and fragile, like they were made of porcelain. But before their hands could fully connect, Manny's eyes flashed bright like a bolt of lightning, and Lucely shielded her face with her free arm.

When she opened her eyes, she was surrounded by trees, a starless sky stretching out above her. "Manny?" She looked around, but no one was there. She took a tentative step through the brush, and a willow tree appeared in the clearing ahead. Not just any tree, but *her* tree. She turned around, but her house wasn't there. Instead, greenery encompassed her, twisting and blooming everywhere she looked. It was as if the forest was not just alive but breathing, trying to reach out for her. Trees and wild bushes formed a small enclosure, a grove that seemed separated from the world.

But still Lucely felt in her heart that this place was connected to her home.

"Where am I?" she asked. Her voice was small and afraid.

"You're home," a familiar voice said.

"Manny! Are you okay?"

"He's fine for now." Macarena's voice came to her, loud at first before fading away, stretched thin like a piece of taffy.

"But we won't be if they're not stopped." Manny was beside Lucely once more, back to his old self and not scary like he was in the kitchen moments before.

"What are you talking about? Who are *they*?" Lucely asked.

Manny nodded toward the willow tree, and Lucely watched as fireflies flew in ribbons of light around it, before going out all at once.

"Where'd they—"

"Watch." Tía Milagros appeared beside Lucely, one hand on her shoulder. "And don't be afraid. This is from a time that has already passed."

The moment she'd finished speaking, a roar ripped through the air, the blue sky churning until it was so dark it seemed to be made of ink. Lucely shrank back, fear clawing at every cell in her body. Everything about this moment was impossible.

From the darkness, a creature emerged, a monstrous shadowy thing that made the willow tree look like a bush in comparison. Its body and limbs seemed to be made of a murky white mist. Where its mouth and eyes should've been there were gaping black voids.

Lucely opened her mouth to scream but stopped when she felt the firm yet calming grip of Tía Milagros's bony hand on her shoulder.

The monster circled the tree, planning its next move. It clawed at the bark and howled, bringing its hand back against its chest as if it were burned. The monster tried to shake the tree and throw a boulder at it, but an invisible force kept all its attacks at bay. Finally, the monster began to run laps around the tree, picking up speed until it was enveloped in what looked like . . . like a hurricane. The willow stood steadfast, untouched in the eye of the storm, as the monster grew in size and strength.

Wind and rain whipped around Lucely and her ghost family, stinging her skin and blowing her hair back, but they stood firm too. Lucely knew this was something she was meant to witness. And though the raging wind and her own fear were fighting against her, trying with all their might to pin her to the ground, she would not budge.

The willow tree shook so violently that Lucely feared it might crack right down the middle, as if struck by lightning.

Then a vibrant yellow-and-orange light began to bloom from within the maelstrom, spreading outward until it enveloped the tree itself. A legion of voices rang out at once.

"Away, away

We shall not fear.

Away, foul beast,

And far from here!"

The mist monster screamed as it was thrown backward into the brush. As the fight continued, a soft voice found its way out of the masses and wrapped itself around Lucely, warm and comforting like her favorite wool blanket. It was a voice as clear as a church bell, swooping and curling around her like a small, cream-and-brown palmchat in flight. It was a voice she would know anywhere.

"Mamá," Lucely whispered. Her own voice seemed to echo and amplify in the storm, as if it were being carried by magic.

"The spirit of the cocuyos have been here for centuries, mi niña. Protecting our family and St. Augustine from evil spirits who wish to bring nothing but destruction." Mamá's voice whirled around them, like an arrow made of wind and air and light. "Our family is one of just two ancient orders charged with keeping this city and its inhabitants safe. But there is a new danger approaching. One that threatens to take us all, including the living, into the underworld." Mamá appeared before her, unfazed by the monster's attacks.

Just then, the mist monster launched itself from the brush, flames erupting from its mouth.

"Mamá!" Lucely cried out, but the fire seemed to extinguish itself as soon as it reached her abuela. "I'm not strong like you. I'm just a kid. How am I supposed to stop whatever evil is coming?"

"You don't have to do it alone," Mamá said, just as she transformed into a spark of brilliant blue light. The light shot up into the air, and then with a giant *thud* Mamá's spirit, now at least the height of the willow tree, landed next to Lucely, her slippered feet spread apart and her cane cracking the ground beneath her. Her gray hair moved like the waves of the ocean around her wrinkled face. She looked fierce and terrible and powerful. The mist monster cowered behind a bush, its fire reduced to ash. And Mamá floated toward Lucely.

"You don't have to do it alone because we are with you, always." Mamá ran one giant finger along Lucely's cheek and smiled. "*I* am with you always." Mamá returned to her normal size and placed one hand on Lucely's heart. "Here."

The trees surrounding Lucely began to blend together until the entire scene looked like a Van Gogh painting. An instant later, Lucely was back in her kitchen where her cousin lay motionless on the floor.

"Manny!" Lucely ran over and knelt down next to him. She reached out a hand to feel for a heartbeat before remembering that he hadn't had one for ten years. All she could do was sit and wait.

Five minutes passed, and Manny still didn't wake up. Tears filled Lucely's eyes as she thought that she'd lost her cousin forever.

Manny groaned as he strained to move. "That was weird."

Lucely bolted to attention. "Are you okay? Did . . . did you see that mist monster thing too?"

"Yeah, but I'm not sure how. Or why. I just felt angry. Like pure rage was flowing through my veins." Manny sat up, his hands shaking. "It was like something was controlling me. I'm sorry, Luce. I didn't mean to scare you."

"I'm just glad you're okay." Lucely wrapped her arms around her cousin and squeezed tightly. "You could never really scare me, Manny. No matter what weirdo things you do."

Manny laughed, pushing her away in mock offense.

"But what did Mamá mean when she said that our family is 'one of two ancient orders' protecting St. Augustine? And why is this happening now?"

"I don't know, Luce. But you heard Mamá. Something evil

is coming." The look in Manny's eyes was one of fear, the same look Mamá had had right before she went haywire.

Lucely shivered. Though she would never admit it to Manny, whatever was happening terrified her, and she was ashamed.

"Don't worry, cuz. I'm going to find a way to fix this."

CHAPTER SIX

LUCELY CHECKED HER WATCH for the seven-hundredth time as she waited at the end of her street. It was 9:52 p.m., and Syd still hadn't shown up. She bit her lip, wondering if she'd gotten caught sneaking out. But Syd was slicker than any kid or adult Lucely knew. There was no way she'd gotten caught if Lucely hadn't.

A few more minutes passed, and despite the light chill in the air, Lucely started to sweat. At least she wasn't totally alone out there. Her cousin Macarena flew around inside the mason jar Lucely had attached to her bike. When she had told the fireflies of their plan, Macarena jumped at the chance to join them on their late-night escapade. Even as a ghost, her FOMO was real.

The cemetery was close—just a few minutes walk—but the thought of going without Syd was too scary, especially after what she'd seen lately. And without the key, she had no way of getting into Anastasia's mausoleum.

Lucely furrowed her brow, trying to think of a backup plan, when Syd's bike finally screeched to a halt next to her.

"What took you so long?!" Lucely asked.

"My dad was practicing for an upcoming concert, so it took him longer to go to bed than usual. Mom, on the other hand, was snoring before the saxophone even reached his lips," Syd joked.

Lucely snorted. "Let's go before it gets any later. I don't want to run into Babette when she's got the late-night munchies."

A solitary lamp stood at the entrance of the cove where Babette's house tucked itself away from the rest of the world. It looked like a completely different place in the dark. A sign reading A WITCH LIVES HERE had been nailed to a tree with the words *Babette's Baubles* scribbled beneath. Beyond the sign, the house stood in the middle of a swampy lake, a twisted shadow of a structure that seemed to be craning its neck to snoop on the woods surrounding it. It looked almost like a creepy black-and-white movie come to life, except for the solitary splash of color—Babette's purple front door.

"I hate this," Lucely said. "It's so much creepier at night."

"Come on. It's just Babette's." Syd's voice was confident, but Lucely knew by the way she kept touching her braids that she was scared too.

"We're going to have to take the footbridge," Lucely said.

"No way!" Syd shot Lucely a horrified look. "I am *not* going over that thing at night."

"Look, we have to sneak into Babette's house one way or another to get the key to the mausoleum. And if we take the rowboat, we'll be caught for sure. That is, if we don't flip over and *drown* in the dead of night first. Plus, that swamp gives me the willies."

Syd raised one finger and opened her mouth to argue, but Lucely jumped back in before she could say anything.

"*And* if we have to make a break for it, we'll have to row back across so Babette won't notice the boat is on the wrong shore. It would be a lot simpler to just creep across the footbridge."

"If we fall in, I'm telling Babette you hypnotized me."

"Fine." Lucely smiled triumphantly. It wasn't easy to win an argument with Syd.

"I don't know why mausoleums need locks anyway. It's not like people are *dying* to break in."

Lucely shook her head before cracking a smile. "Okay, that one was pretty good."

They leaned their bikes against a tree and crept toward the footbridge.

"You go first," Syd whispered.

"I'm *shocked* that you'd sacrifice me like this. I thought we were friends."

"It was *your* idea to take this cursed path," Syd protested.

Both girls kept their voices low.

"Let's go across together at least," Lucely said.

"Fine, you owe me so much, I hope you know that."

They held hands as they stepped onto the bridge together.

"I guess this is how I go," Syd muttered. But despite the bridge being super old and creaky, they got across without incident.

Lucely let out a sigh of relief. "See?"

"Yeah, yeah. Come on before Babette's witchy senses wake her up."

Syd found the spare key Babette kept hidden beneath a frog statuette that had been enchanted to look and, unfortunately, feel real.

Once inside, they crept toward the library. Lucely said a silent prayer that the house would be too tired to play any tricks on them tonight. The light from Syd's phone reflected off a mirror, causing them both to jump, thinking they'd for sure been caught.

A low, clipped *meow* came from the hallway, and Lucely and Syd spun around in tandem.

"It's just Chunk," Lucely whispered. "Come here, girl."

Lucely held her hand out, and Chunk shuffled toward her.

"Meow?"

"We're just looking for a key, Chunk," Syd said.

Even though Chunk was a cat and couldn't understand what they were saying, Lucely and Syd always spoke to her as if she were human.

Chunk collapsed dramatically on Lucely's feet and looked up. "Meow." This time her cry seemed to hold a warning.

"No time for your ominous meowing, Chunk," Syd said.

Lucely tried to pull away, but Chunk had now wrapped her body around Lucely's legs.

"I can't move," Lucely said.

"Just keep her occupied. I'll find the keys," Syd said, turning the corner up ahead.

Chunk began howling now, and Lucely tried her best to calm her down.

"Hurry, Syd," Lucely pleaded, hoping Babette was a deep sleeper.

Sweat trickled down Lucely's forehead, her stomach doing somersaults.

A few moments later Syd returned.

"I couldn't find the keys," she told Lucely. "Babette must have moved them."

Chunk sauntered out of the room, immediately disinterested in them, probably to find a box to squeeze into and sleep. Syd quirked an eyebrow knowingly in the cat's direction.

"I think I hear footsteps coming from upstairs. We have to go before Babette sees us." Syd took Lucely's hand, and as quietly as they could manage, they bolted out the door.

The front door flew open, and Babette stood on her porch, an elegant shadow. Lucely and Syd had run as far as they could without a light and crouched behind a giant bush to catch their breath.

"Whoever you are, you don't know who and what you're messing with," Babette warned. Her voice carried in the night air, commanding and threatening. "Babette Faires will be your thorn."

All around them they could see the garden coming to life, thorny vines whipping and striking at the air. The sound of the door slamming shut propelled them both out from behind the bush and across the footbridge. Lucely had never run faster in her life.

By the time they reached the other side of the cove, both girls were out of breath and shaking.

"We almost *died*," Syd said.

"And all for nothing." Lucely replied.

"Not for *nothing*." Syd smirked, reaching into her pocket and pulling out a ring of large, rusty skeleton keys.

"I thought you said you couldn't find—"

"Chunk was being weird. I swear sometimes I think she's Babette's spy. Better to be safe than sorry. Come on, before I change my mind about disturbing the dead."

When Lucely and Syd made it to the cemetery, the moon was directly overhead, casting an eerie glow over the McMaster family mausoleum in front of them.

"I'm not opening it." Syd handed the keys to Lucely.

"First, the footbridge, and now this? I'm beginning to question our friendship." Lucely shook her head. Above the ancient marble doors were some words that looked like Latin. She hoped they weren't some sort of curse.

Lucely tried several keys before the right one clicked into place, opening the door with a sound that reminded her of her tío Fernando attempting to get out of his recliner.

It was cooler inside the mausoleum than outside in the humid Florida heat. Even at night the air was almost unbearable. As soon as they entered the room, a pungent odor filled Lucely's nostrils. It smelled like dirty gym socks and moldy cheese, and she had to hold her breath to keep from barfing.

The light from their cell phones reflected off the marble walls, illuminating a row of square headstones on the back wall, each marked with the name of a deceased family member.

"Okay then, do the thing." Syd flailed her hands.

"What *thing*?"

"I don't know?! Find Anastasia's coffin and look inside? This was your idea!"

"No way! I am not sticking my hand inside a coffin!"

"Then why did we even come here?"

Lucely sighed, hating that Syd was right. If they had any hope of finding the missing pages, they had to look *everywhere*.

Together, they stepped up to Anastasia's casket and shifted the heavy lid aside just enough for Lucely to reach down and run her hands along the inner walls of the coffin. The smooth marble felt like silk on Lucely's hands. Then her fingers grazed against rough stone.

"Wait, I may have found something," Lucely said, breathless.

Syd shone what little light she could through the gap where Lucely's hand had been. "I can't really see anything in there."

Lucely plunged her arm back into the dark space. "Let me see if I can shimmy whatever it is free from the wall."

A cloud of dust erupted as she pulled the rough-hewn stone from its place, and both girls jumped back, waving their hands wildly and coughing.

"Gross, dead-people dust," said Syd.

When the air finally cleared, the empty space where the stone had once sat was now visible. A rolled-up piece of paper peeked out from the space behind the stone. They looked at each other, mouths open. "Is that—"

But before Syd could finish, Lucely had reached in and grabbed the paper, settling onto the cool marble bench nearby.

Syd moved to join her, holding up her light as Lucely delicately unrolled the parchment.

"I think it's in Latin or something." Lucely ran her eyes over the odd words and symbols. She turned the paper over, but there was nothing on the other side. "Maybe we could try translating it on our phones?"

As soon as Lucely had said the words, the inscription began to change. Like a puff of smoke passing over the paper, the once illegible words were now all in English.

"Whoa," said Syd.

Lucely gulped as she read the first few words on the paper aloud: "A Spell to Wake the Sleeping."

"You think this might be one of the missing pages from the spell book?"

Lucely extracted the book from inside her jacket, opened it to the back, and compared the piece of paper to the torn edges in the book. It was a match.

This was it. Lucely looked to Syd, who cleared her throat in response.

"Hold on. I have an idea. Point the flashlight at the floor." Syd took a piece of white chalk from her pocket and drew a large pentagram on the floor. Of course, Syd knew how to draw a perfect pentagram. When she had finished, they both sat down in the middle of the magical symbol, the concrete ground cold beneath them.

Lucely shivered. "Maybe this is a bad idea. I mean, what if something goes wrong?"

Syd sighed. "Luce, it's either this or nothing. You want to save your fireflies, don't you? We can't chicken out now."

Lucely turned it over in her mind. There really wasn't anything else she could think to do, especially now that they were here with a possible answer in their hands. She nodded at Syd and said a silent prayer that things would work out.

"Together." Syd took hold of Lucely's hands as they began to read the rest of the inscription aloud.

"Lavender, lilies, blossom and bloom,
I call on the spirits to enter this room . . ."

They paused and looked around. Fear had been creeping up on Lucely since she'd left her house, and now it was raging.

"Rotten and putrid
Beneath the trees,
I call on the spirits and let them roam free."

Lucely held her breath, Syd's hands tightening around hers.

They waited one minute. Then another.

A strong breeze swept through the room, chilling Lucely to the bone, but aside from that, nothing particularly *magical* seemed to happen.

"Maybe check on Macarena?" said Syd.

Lucely unclipped the small mason jar from her backpack and tapped gently on the glass. "Maca?"

Macarena flew out of the jar, appearing before Lucely, and yawned.

"Everything okay, Luce?" she asked.

Lucely hesitated. "Do you feel anything different with Mamá's spirit?"

Her cousin closed her eyes and took a deep breath, letting it out slowly. "Sorry, prima. It feels the same as it was before."

Lucely sighed, fighting back tears. So the spell to wake the sleeping hadn't worked to heal Mamá and the rest of the firefly spirits. "Thanks for trying. You can go back to sleep now."

Macarena shrugged sleepily before transforming back into a firefly and settling at the bottom of her jar.

"Huh, that's weird. I didn't see this on the paper before." Syd pointed at two letters that had appeared: E. B.

"What do you think it means?" Lucely asked.

Syd shrugged. "Could be the initials of the witch that created the spell?"

"Well, whoever it was must not have been very good at magic." Lucely tucked the useless paper into the spell book. They waited a while longer, hoping for some other sign that the spell had worked. But when it was obvious that nothing was going to happen, they made their way out of the mausoleum.

Lucely and Syd felt defeated as they walked back to their bikes.

A *crack* sounded from somewhere behind them.

"Get down, shh," Lucely whispered, diving behind a nearby gravestone.

A shadowy figure stalked across the cemetery and toward the mausoleum where Lucely and Syd had just been, seemingly oblivious to their presence.

"Is that . . . Mayor Anderson?" Syd asked.

The figure was becoming clearer in the moonlight: a ridiculously tall man, hunched over, a long, fluffy handlebar mustache hanging from his face. It certainly *looked* like Mayor Anderson.

"What is the mayor doing creeping around the cemetery in the middle of the night?" asked Syd.

Lucely gave her a grim look, and they both turned their attention back to the entrance of the mausoleum, waiting for him to come out.

Moments later, he emerged. Something seemed different about him. It was almost as if he were floating instead of walking, but in jerky, unstable motions.

His gaze shifted in their direction, locking in on their hiding place as if he could see them through the darkness.

Lucely held back a scream when she noticed Mayor Anderson's eyes, which were now glowing an unnatural green.

CHAPTER SEVEN

LUCELY STRUGGLED TO KEEP her eyes open as she sat in the school library the next day waiting for Syd to arrive. She hadn't gotten home until after one in the morning the previous night, and she thanked whatever saint was looking over her that her dad hadn't woken up. What little sleep she had been able to get was interrupted by nightmares of corpses breaking out of their graves, the words of the spell running on repeat in her mind, and the sickly green glow of Mayor Anderson's eyes.

The school day had passed by in a haze of yawns and eye rubbing. Lucely even tried splashing her face with cold water in the bathroom, but that didn't seem to help. She wanted nothing more than to go home and take the longest nap in the history of naps. But after what she'd seen in the cemetery, she was even more determined to find something that would help the firefly spirits and her dad.

A few of her classmates were goofing around nearby, and Tilly Maxwell, who seemed to hate Lucely for no good reason, pointed at Lucely's sneakers and whispered something to a girl next to her. They erupted in laughter before walking away.

Her sneakers had been white once, but despite her scrubbing them with an old toothbrush and washing her shoelaces, now they were pretty much falling apart. There was even a hole on the side that hadn't been there that morning. Lucely buried her face in the book she was holding, wishing the earth would swallow her whole.

Just as Lucely was about to fall asleep, using her book as a pillow, Syd strode into the room and sat down with a huff. "Sorry, sorry, sorry. Band practice went late. Andy got his lips stuck in the tuba again."

Lucely yawned in response.

"Wake up, Luce! You're gonna want to see this." Syd pulled Babette's book, *Magic and the Occult: A History*, out of her backpack and flipped it open to a section she'd flagged. "I was scanning through it in study hall when I came across this passage."

Syd began to read aloud while Lucely followed along.

"Las Brujas Moradas, or the Purple Coven, was a well-known coven from Logroño, Spain.

"During the Spanish Inquisition, their oldest member, Alanza, was accused of being a witch. The coven attempted to fight back, but the village ran them out, so the coven fled to the small coastal city of St. Augustine, Florida. They spent their days caring for the sick of St. Augustine and helping bring new life into the world as well as protecting the city from . . ."

Syd looked at Lucely, her eyes wide.

"What, what, Syd?" Lucely nearly tipped over in her seat.

"As well as protecting the city from dangerous and malicious spirits."

The weight of the words sent Lucely slumping back into her chair. Mamá had mentioned something about there being another ancient order served with protecting St. Augustine. Could she have been referring to Las Brujas Moradas?

Syd continued to read.

"Many townspeople believed that the Purple Coven had a book of magic filled with curses and hexes, while others believed it was the source of their power and the very thing that protected their city. The book is said to contain the most powerful of magical spells, including healing, love, and . . . resurrection."

Syd paused before she read the next part, "The last known documentation of such a book existing claimed that it had been buried somewhere in the Tolomato Cemetery. To this day no book has ever been found."

"*Omg,*" Lucely said as Syd closed the book. "Do you think . . ."

"It *has* to be," said Syd. "Babette said she'd found this book in the cemetery, remember? Maybe she found the spell book there too!"

"But we *tried* one of the spells already, and it didn't work."

"That doesn't mean that there aren't others hidden around town. If we keep searching, I'm sure we'll be able to find more clues that will lead us in the right direction."

"But we don't have time for a scavenger hunt, Syd! It could take us weeks, or months, or even *years*, to find the spell we need. I don't know how long my fireflies can keep holding on."

Syd wrapped her arms around Lucely, pulling her into a hug as tears began to wet her eyes. "If there's anyone who could find the spell, it would be the two of us, Luce. Magic or no magic, I will always be right by your side. We're a team."

Lucely knew that Syd was right. If they had any chance of bringing Mamá back, of making sure her spirit family was okay, they had no choice but to track down the rest of the missing pages.

"You're right. We have to find the spell, Syd," Lucely said, more determined than ever. "But you know we can't do this alone. You're not gonna like this but . . ."

Syd gave Lucely a probing look.

"Babette is the only one who can help us. She's probably hiding an encyclopedic knowledge of magic in her hair or something."

Syd crossed her arms in front of her chest. "My answer is still no way. Not unless you plan on pulling double dusting duty when she inevitably punishes us for meddling again."

Before Lucely had a chance to respond, to beg for Syd's help, the windows of the library blew open with a loud crash, sending papers flying and causing Syd and Lucely to scream in unison.

When Lucely had gotten to the library earlier in the afternoon, there wasn't a cloud in the sky. Now the sky was blotted out with menacing black clouds. Wind and rain raged in through the open library windows louder than Tía Milagros after someone made a mess in the house.

The hair on Lucely's arms stood on end. Something wasn't right.

She collapsed to the ground, gasping for air as the memory of the fire-breathing mist monster consumed her. *Something bad is coming. It's coming with the rain.*

As quickly as the memory came, it vanished. Lucely's vision slowly returned to the room. It felt as if she was being pulled from the depths of the ocean toward the surface. By the time Syd's face had come into focus, Lucely could tell by her expression that whatever had just happened terrified her.

Mr. Castañeda, the school librarian, ran into the room to see what all the commotion was about. "Are you girls okay? I've never seen a storm like this."

Syd was the first to break eye contact, responding with a nervous laugh. "We're fine, Mr. C. Just a bit of wind and rain."

He got to work trying to close the windows, but they refused to budge. Mr. Castañeda was soaked in seconds. A fog began to roll into the room, moving toward them like a fox on the hunt, but only Lucely and Syd seemed to notice it.

"Lucely Luna." A haunting voice cut through the howling wind and seemed to whisper in their ears.

"What was that? Who's speaking?" Syd's question was met with no response.

"We should probably get out of here," Lucely shouted.

Mr. Castañeda finally surrendered. "I'm going to go get the janitor. Maybe he can help me close these windows. You girls shouldn't go out in this storm. Wait here."

The moment Mr. Castañeda was gone, they heard what sounded like footsteps behind one of the stacks.

"This isn't funny," Syd called out. "Quit hiding and show yourself!"

Syd wielded a large book above her head while Lucely clung on to Syd's backpack as they inched closer to the noise.

"Hello?" Syd called out, and this time something answered.

A chorus of low moans echoed throughout the room, vibrating the very air around them. Lucely pulled Syd back as she swung the book wildly into the air, screaming.

"Come on!" Lucely said.

They broke into a run just as one of the bookshelves came crashing down where they had been standing.

Transparent figures glided across the floor, arms out-stretched toward Lucely and Syd. Their movements were jerky and unnatural. These were nothing like the spirits Lucely had grown up with—these were monsters. They looked like smaller versions of the fire-breathing mist monster from her vision, with gaping, black holes where their eyes and mouths should've been.

"Syd, keep moving!" Lucely grabbed Syd's hand and ran faster than she had in her entire life.

"What are those things?!" Syd's voice quivered with disbelief.

The air was frigid, causing goose bumps to form all over Lucely's body. A smell like dead mice and ancient earth filled the room as the ghosts attempted to surround them.

"What now?" she asked.

"This way." Syd pulled Lucely under a low arch in the section where the kindergarten class had reading time.

Lucely's calves ached. They were running in circles trying to avoid the ghosts, but they weren't getting any closer to the exit.

"LUCELY LUNA!" the voices boomed from every corner of the library as Lucely pulled Syd into a small alcove.

"How do they know your name?" Syd asked, clearly terrified.

Lucely shook with fear. "I don't want to think about that right now. We have to find a way to distract them long enough to escape."

"Can they even be distracted?"

"No idea, but it's worth a shot. And I have a plan."

After filling Syd in, Lucely dropped down to all fours, crawling as quietly as she could until she reached a row of the old computers they used during design class. Going down the line as quickly as she could, she pressed the power button on every tower. Syd was doing the same on the opposite side of the library.

Once she was finished, Lucely looked around to make sure the coast was clear. She could hear the ghosts wailing somewhere near the sci-fi section. They swept the floor with their blank faces and sunken black voids for eyes. She looked across the library to her left, where Syd was standing waiting for her signal. She nodded, and they took off at a sprint toward the door, hoping their plan would work.

As Lucely approached the last set of bookshelves, one of the monsters materialized directly in front of her, blocking her path.

Lucely came to a sudden halt, frozen with fear.

"*Lucelyyyy,*" the monster hissed. "*Come with meeee . . .*"

She couldn't move, though she wanted to. Couldn't scream, though she was trying to. All Lucely could do was close her eyes and pray that she would make it out of there alive.

The evil spirit growled at her, a horrifying expression of glee on its face. The gaping maw where its mouth should've been stretched across its face in some terrible mimic of a smile.

Then, in a voice made of nightmares, it began to sing.

"*Duermase, mi niña. Duermase, mi amor . . .*"

A scream caught in Lucely's throat. It felt as if the monster were ripping her spirit right out of her body as it sang the very lullaby Mamá always sang to her. Her eyes were becoming heavy, and despite the fear hammering in her heart, she knew she was moments from losing consciousness and falling into the clutches of the monster.

"LUCELY!" Syd's voice cut through the haze just as the computers finished booting up, blasting the Windows intro music throughout the library at full volume.

Lucely snapped out of the trance, in a stupor. The monster that just moments before had been sucking the very life out of her fled toward the center of the room, where the horde of evil spirits were descending on the computers like a tornado in a flurry of howls and mist.

Lucely ran to Syd, who was standing by the exit, and together they burst through the doors and into the rain, grabbing their bikes and peddling away from the library as fast as they could. When they finally stopped, so had the wind and rain. Syd hopped off her bike and collapsed onto a patch of grass, not caring that it was wet since they were both already soaked through.

"What . . . just . . . happened?" Syd asked, still trying to catch her breath.

"We almost got poltergeisted, that's *what*! And I think one of them was trying give me some sort of Dementor's Kiss." Lucely tried not to burst into tears. "Syd, this is bad, real bad. Whatever just happened—whatever those things were—I'm almost positive that it was entirely our fault."

CHAPTER EIGHT

"MAMÁ." LUCELY CUPPED her grandmother's mason jar in her hands. "Mamá, despierta."

She examined Mamá's tiny firefly, hoping for some kind of sign, but Mamá still didn't stir. Not even her wings fluttered now.

Lucely sat down at the base of the willow tree, defeated. Absolutely everything was upside down. She was losing her family's home, Mamá was . . . gone, and now she and Syd may have accidentally been responsible for the arrival of those evil phantoms at the library.

Lucely hid her face in her hands and let the tears come. She had never felt so alone.

"¿Y esa lloradera?" A shrill voice floated down from one

of the top branches. Small at first, then louder as it got closer.

"¿Qué te pasa?" Tía Milagros sat next to Lucely on the ground, looking uncomfortable. This tía was not the type to sit on the grass and chat. Her hobbies were more akin to a neighborhood gossip, always perched on a rocking chair or peeking through the blinds, tutting her teeth at everyone and everything. When she wasn't cleaning, that is. She made the best pastelitos though—the kind with ground beef and scrambled eggs—so she wasn't all bad.

"Do you know what's wrong with Mamá?" Lucely wiped her eyes and sniffed.

Tía Milagros's face was in a perpetual scowl that served only to enhance the curlers and face mask that she passed away in and were now her permanent state of being. But upon Lucely's question, her face softened. Then her expression turned grave.

She sighed. "I'm not sure. I have never seen this happen before. Even when I was a young girl," Tía Milagros said in a heavy accent.

Lucely hesitated before gathering the courage to tell her about the spell she and Syd had found in the cemetery. "We were just trying to help. Do you think we might have made things worse?"

Tía Milagros reached for Lucely's hand. "No, no, mija. I do not know what is happening, but I do know that no child is capable of this . . . brujeria. This is dark magic. The storm is bringing something with it, something evil. Every day we feel it growing stronger. And Mamá's not the only one affected by it. I feel it in the air, heavy on my bones. On all our bones. Like we are being stretched too thin."

"Manny," Lucely said, remembering her cousin's fit the other night and the terrifying vision that followed.

"Manny, Mamá, Tío Elido. Me. We've all been having nightmares." Tía Milagros's voice was small, afraid.

Lucely gasped, and despite the suffocating heat, a shiver took over her limbs.

"It's like we're reliving our own deaths, and then, everything after. Everything you are spared from enduring when you cross over. All the pain and tears of our family and our loved ones." Tía Milagros clutched her locket, which Lucely knew had a picture of her children and husband, all still alive and living in New York. "It's painless to die, Lucely. It's peaceful. What hurts the most is watching those you loved in life mourn you in death. It's enough to break a heart. Even one as hard as mine."

Lucely threw her arms around her tía. "I don't know what to do. How to help."

Her world seemed to be crumbling around her like a

week-old cookie she'd left in her pocket. How could she fix this? Where would she even begin?

"I'll talk to the others, see if they have any ideas," Tía Milagros said. "We Lunas are not the giving-up type. You have your father's spirit in you, all our spirits. You are the only one who can stop this, Lucely. We believe in you."

CHAPTER NINE

LUCELY AVOIDED BUSES whenever she could—the tough material covering the seats always reeked of caked-in sweat and burnt plastic—but her class trip to city hall was their best opportunity to spy on Mayor Anderson to see what he was really up to. Lucely was sure she had seen him that night in the cemetery. They had to find out if he was connected to the ghosts somehow.

Syd had saved Lucely the window seat because she knew how sick she got on buses.

"Ready to be spies?" Syd whispered, wiggling her cycbrows.

Lucely smiled. "Yep. Got my dad's tape recorder from his dresser last night. Good thing he sleeps like a rock."

They went over their plan in hushed voices, heads together for the entire drive.

City hall was an extravagant building, with a giant fountain and perfectly manicured gardens out front. It reminded Lucely of pictures she'd seen of the architecture in Spain with its terra-cotta roofs.

Rain was coming down in sheets as the class poured out of the bus in their school-issue yellow ponchos. They looked like ducklings following Mr. Lopez into the building as he went over the rules. Everyone had a buddy to keep them from wandering off for any reason.

Lucely had no issue adhering to the buddy system, since she and Syd did that even when it wasn't required. The not-wandering-off part? Not so much. She threw Syd a knowing look as they filed into the building, making sure to stick to the back near the class aide. Mrs. Stein was nice enough, but she was also, like, ninety-eight years old, and they had a much better chance of giving her the slip than Mr. Lopez.

Lucely and Syd followed their class around for nearly an hour, nodding along and pretending to be interested in the rich history of their city when really they were thinking of the best way to get up to the government offices without getting caught. Mr. Lopez wouldn't be doing another head count until lunch, and then they'd be wrapping up their tour with a meet-and-greet with the mayor right before they went home. If they were going to have any chance of picking up something juicy, they needed to record for a few hours. They had to go now.

"Bathroom break!" Mr. Lopez called from the front of the line, and Lucely knew this might be their only chance.

"Okay," she whispered to Syd. "He'll do another count after the bathroom break, and then we make a run for it."

"Got it," Syd said.

They waited for the rest of their classmates to take their bathroom breaks and line up again.

Once Mr. Lopez had done another count, and just as they passed the staircase that would take them to the mayor's office, Lucely and Syd slipped into an open janitor's closet.

They peered out from the cracked door, crossing their fingers that they hadn't been caught. Mrs. Stein stopped, looking confused for a moment, before shrugging and continuing.

"That was close." Lucely let out a breath.

"The wrath of Mrs. Stein has been avoided again."

"God forbid she knit us a cozy sweater!" Lucely shuddered.

Syd laughed and put a hand on Lucely's shoulder. "You've gotta work on your jokes, Luce."

They both laughed as they ran up the stairs and toward the mayor's office.

Lucely had no idea if he would even be in there, but this might be their only chance to figure out *how* he was involved before it was too late.

Palm trees lurched outside the office windows, threatening to snap in the howling winds as the storm continued to rage. Lucely rubbed her arms. The AC was blasting, and that— combined with being out in the rain earlier—made for a chilly situation. She was sick of rain.

When they got upstairs, Syd smiled and nodded at the adults she passed in the hallway as if she belonged there. They probably thought they were someone's kids, because nobody stopped to ask them what they were doing there.

The mayor's office was at the end of the hall, between two giant ferns. On the door was one of those envelopes where people put mail. Lucely hoped the microphone on the recorder was strong enough to pick up sound from inside it.

She looked over to Syd, who was busy loitering in front of Mayor Anderson's secretary.

"Now," she mouthed, and Syd nodded in response.

"Hi, I'm lost. Can you help me?" Syd asked the secretary.

A look of panic came over the older man's face as he sig-naled for Syd to sit down and began asking her questions. Lucely made her move over to the mayor's office, pressed her ear to the door, and heard a deep voice inside. She stepped back quickly so she wouldn't attract any suspicion.

He was definitely in there.

Lucely looked back at Syd before slipping the recorder into the large envelope on the door, making sure the little red light indicating it was on lit up before she did. Then she turned around and went straight for Syd.

"Cinderella!" Lucely whispered. Syd snorted at the code name she had insisted on.

"I've been looking all over for you. Mr. Lopez asked me to come find you."

The man at the desk looked visibly relieved, wiping beads of sweat from his bald head. "You two get back to your teacher now," he said. Lucely nodded, taking Syd by the hand as they ran down the hall. Now they just had to wait.

They found their class just as they were walking into the cafeteria for lunch. Lucely slid in right behind Mrs. Stein and coughed as Syd took a sip of water from a fountain right next to her. Mrs. Stein just smiled at them sweetly and shuffled out the door toward the rest of the class. She had seen them, which would be enough, Lucely hoped, to make her think they had been there the entire time.

After lunch, Lucely followed her classmates down the hallway of offices she had walked past an hour before. She could feel every nerve in her body buzzing.

Mr. Lopez gestured toward a man who looked to be about nine hundred years old. "This is where you pay a parking ticket.

"And this is where you get a marriage license," he said, introducing the class to a woman who was chewing gum and looking down like she could actually see the germs on the children's faces.

When they eventually reached the end of the hallway, Mayor Anderson slipped out from his office like an eel. He was tall—much taller than he looked on television—and wore a beige trench coat and the shiniest shoes Lucely had ever seen.

"Welcome, class, *ahem*. I am Mayor Anderson and . . ."

Lucely watched intently as he droned on. There was something off about him. It was almost as if the words coming from his mouth didn't match up with his lips moving, like he was in a badly dubbed movie or something. She shivered, remembering the thing that had looked like him in the cemetery. Sure, he seemed kind of weird, but not like a giant mist monster. Not even close.

Maybe they were wrong about him, Lucely thought briefly. Those monsters couldn't be the same as the person standing before them now, could they?

"Come in, come in. Don't be shy." The mayor flourished his arm in an exaggerated gesture, and the class trickled into his office cautiously. Lucely tried to lag behind to see if she could snatch the recorder quickly, but the mayor was still standing at the door, smiling down at her.

Lucely chuckled nervously and ducked into the office. Syd was nowhere to be found. The mayor swept into the office and stood behind his desk, gesturing for Lucely to join the rest of her class, which had gathered in front of it. Lucely chanced one more look out the door behind her, but Syd wasn't there. She had been with her just a moment ago. Reluctantly, she joined her classmates, craning her neck every few seconds to look for Syd.

A few minutes later, Syd sauntered into the office with Mrs. Stein in tow.

"She had to use the ladies' room and couldn't find the right door," she told Mr. Lopez as Syd rejoined the class.

Syd winked at Lucely, patting the side pocket on her jacket casually.

Lucely suppressed an excited smile. The rest of the class trip was an agonizing wait until they were back on the school bus, where they could listen to the recorder undisturbed.

They made sure to be the last students to board so that they'd get to sit up front where no one would ask them what they were listening to. Lucely had brought a headphone splitter so they could both listen at the same time.

At first there was nothing but static. Long stretches of it, broken up only by the occasional person coughing or speaking unintelligibly. Then Lucely thought she heard something muffled. She turned it up, and that's when the voices started. Not just one or two—it was at least three people speaking in hushed tones and quick whispers.

"The plan is in motion," a scratchy, high-pitched voice said.

"We've only collected fifty so far, which is by no means enough!" responded another voice—this one sounded like it had a cold.

"Quiet. Do you want that bumbling secretary outside to find us out?" Mayor Anderson said.

"Pah!" Lucely couldn't tell if this was in response to the mayor or if the second voice had just sneezed.

"You must continue to collect them and avoid that witch and her annoying assistants," the mayor said. "Or better yet, capture them if we can. They would make excellent additions. Especially the cat."

Murmurs of agreement resounded, and Lucely looked at Syd who wore the same startled expression she was sure she wore herself. *Witch and her assistants* and *cats*. The voices were talking about *them*.

"When will we know it's time?" asked voice two.

"I cannot believe you have forgotten again," said the mayor with a sigh. "We must collect enough souls before the full moon on Halloween, and then at the stroke of midnight, when the whole town is distracted by the Halloween Festival, we complete the ritual. Then we will outnumber them, and the town will be ours to control."

One of the voices sounded just like Mayor Anderson, that was for certain, but who were the others?

"We mustn't forget about that dreadful firefly tree," said the second voice.

"That is the most important part of all. Their magic has already begun to fade—soon they'll no longer be able to protect the town."

Lucely grabbed Syd's hand tightly just as the recording stopped. Out of battery.

"What are we gonna do?" asked Lucely in a daze. They knew about her tree. About her ancestors. Whoever was in that office was behind whatever was happening to her family.

CHAPTER TEN

"**I HAVE AN IDEA,**" Syd said, digging her toes into the cool grass beneath the willow tree in Lucely's backyard, the fireflies flickering overhead. "You said that the fireflies could sense something was off, right? And they're supposed to protect you."

Lucely nodded, her eyes narrowing. She didn't like the look on Syd's face.

"What if . . . we took a few of them with us—ones that haven't been affected by the storm—and use their spirit energy to try and help us take down some of the ghosts all over town?"

Lucely shook her head. "No way. I won't put them in any more danger."

Syd sighed. "Well, we have to do *something* about the poltergeist problem. You've heard the reports of hauntings all over town. It's only gonna get worse."

"Do you think it has something to do with the full moon being on Halloween this year?" Lucely wondered. "Also, how do you propose we even go about catching ghosts in the first place? You're not about to whip out a working-model proton pack are you?"

"I'm glad you asked." Syd got up and ran into the house. A few moments later, she returned with her backpack. "I made these last night with instructions from the *Phantom Hunters: Amateur Ghost Hunters Manual*." Syd pulled out a mason jar much like the ones in Lucely's willow tree, except this one was tinted a bright green. The lid was painted black and had a few words written on top in white ink. A string connected the latch to the enclosure so that you could close the jar by pulling the latch. The inside of the jar was lined with holographic paper, and a small pouch filled with what looked like oregano hung from a string glued to the inside of the lid. It looked like an art project gone wrong. And it smelled horrible.

"You can't be for real," Lucely said. "You think we're gonna legitimately catch ghosts using glass jars filled with some aluminum foil and Italian herbs? Are you sure you weren't accidentally looking at some weird recipe instead?"

"*Phantom Hunters* swears by them! I might've been a little hasty in the execution, but it's the thought that counts."

Lucely raised an eyebrow. "I'm pretty sure that's for gift giving, not ghost catching."

"Hey! Who's the expert here?"

Lucely raised her hands in mock surrender.

"So, how do my fireflies fit into all this?"

"They can be, like, our signal or whatever. If they start feeling wonky, then we'll know to be on the lookout for nearby ghosts."

"Hmm . . . that's actually pretty brilliant," Lucely said. "I'll have to ask them though. I won't take them against their will."

"Can't argue with that. *And* since your dad is out doing boring dad stuff right now . . ." Syd smiled.

"Okay, okay. I'll talk to them right now." Lucely sighed. "Um . . ." Lucely made a waving gesture at Syd so that she would give her some privacy. She felt weird talking to them around anyone but her dad.

Lucely took a deep breath and looked at her firefly family. Her lips curled into a smile as she thought of Tía Milagros with her chancla in hand, Macarena with her hands on her hips, Mamá with her wrinkled hand on Lucely's shoulder telling her she could do anything. She knew they would tell her to fight.

Macarena appeared on a low bough of the willow, swinging her legs. "Can we bring Frankie? She hasn't stopped talking about the storm or Mamá in *weeks*, and I think she wants to help."

Before Lucely could even say hello, Frankie flew out and shifted from firefly to person in a flurry of light and static. Frankie was a boxer before she passed, and she was really good. Undefeated, in fact. Which was something she *loved* to remind everyone of at every family gathering.

"I've been waiting for you, prima. Let's go!" Frankie bounced from one foot to the other, ready for a match.

"I'm coming too." Tía Milagros appeared, arms crossed and a scowl on her face. Before Lucely could protest, she held on to Macarena's arm with a death grip. Her cousin cringed, and Lucely knew it was no use arguing. "I know the perfect place to start."

Soon after, they had reached their destination. "El Castillo de San Marcos." Lucely waved her hand with a flourish at the stone fortress as if to announce their arrival.

"How are we going to get in?" Syd asked. "They won't let us through without an adult."

"When has that ever stopped us before?" Lucely smirked. "Follow me."

They rode around the perimeter until they found an un-attended gate. Beyond it lay the fortress grounds.

Lucely and Syd chained their bikes to the fence before setting off toward the fortress.

"If anyone asks, pretend we got separated from our parents." Syd winked.

The cool breeze that greeted them as they entered one of the long, narrow passageways inside the fort was a welcome relief from the heat of the day. Lucely was so distracted by the flurry of tourists skittering about, some even whispering excitedly about hoping to see a "real, live ghost," that she'd accidentally tuned out Syd entirely.

"Helloooo . . . Earth to Lucely . . ." Syd waved her hands in the air to grab Lucely's attention. "Did you hear anything I just said?"

"Sorry . . ." Lucely looked apologetic before offering a smile.

"As I was saying," Syd continued, "the *Phantom Hunters* handbook lists the Castillo de San Marcos in its Top Ten Most Haunted Forts in the Southeastern United States—"

"So, what you're *saying*"—Lucely cut in—"is aside from that oddly specific category choice, this place is totally swarming with ghosts. It *has* to be. This place looks older than Babette."

Syd let out a laugh that echoed faintly around them. "If she heard you say that, you'd be a toad already."

As they made their way deeper into the belly of the fortress, the temperature continued to drop, and they suddenly found themselves all alone with nothing but the dark, stone tunnel ahead of them and the light of the fireflies at their sides.

"It's freezing down here." Lucely rubbed her arms. "How much farther?"

No sooner had the words left her lips than the tunnel ahead of them came to an abrupt halt.

"Great," Lucely said. "You'd think there would at least be some spirits hanging out at a *dead* end."

"Still needs some work, but better!" Syd said. "Something does feel a bit *off* down here though."

"Ohhh, are your witchy senses tingling?" Lucely asked, but she felt it too. "I'll check with Macarena to see if she can sense anything."

The moment Lucely removed the lid of the jar, Macarena burst out with a force that knocked Lucely onto her backside.

"Lucely, it's not safe here. You have to go." Macarena looked terrified.

But before Lucely could respond, Syd shouted, "I found something! Come look!"

As Lucely approached Syd, Macarena flew back into the jar, cowering.

"See this stone here . . . and that one there?" Syd pointed to one on either wall directly across from each other. "They're not as grimy as the rest. And, look . . ." She pushed on the one closest to her, and it sank about an inch into the wall.

Lucely gasped. "Do you think it's some sort of Indiana Jones–like mechanism or something?"

"Let's hope it's not a *real* booby trap. I wouldn't stand a chance running away from a three-ton boulder."

"Syd, if there really is something here, don't you think it's a bit too easy?" Lucely asked.

"Shhh, when the universe gives you a gift, you take it and run. Besides, you're not giving me enough credit; maybe I'm just a genius. Now help me with this."

Lucely positioned herself across from Syd before placing her left hand on the frigid stone. She stretched out her right arm and took Syd's hand in hers. "On the count of three?"

"One . . . two . . ."

They both took a deep breath—hoping it wasn't their last—before pressing their full weight against the stones.

Once the dust had cleared, Lucely and Syd could see that a narrow doorway now stood in front of them where before there had only been a solid wall. The room just ahead opened into what looked like an abandoned military barrack. There were clothes and other personal items strewn about, but otherwise it looked almost as if it were untouched since forever ago.

Syd cleared her throat. "What did I say? I'm a genius."

Lucely rolled her eyes and sighed, her breath coming out in a puff of white. "Looks like somebody spoke too soon."

"Don't say I didn't warn you," Macarena said pointedly.

"We stick together." Lucely held her catcher out and signaled for Syd to do the same, before taking a few tentative steps into the room. "There's no telling what kind of ghosts could be hiding down here."

"Well, well, well," the shadows seemed to say in a voice like the barrage of cannon fire from all sides. *"What are two pretty little f-f-finches like yourselves doing so f-f-far from your nest?"*

Out from the darkness stepped a surly man clothed in a centuries-old Spanish militia uniform. His sinister smile betrayed any good intentions, as did the sliver of something white held at his side. With little light to offer any further details, he could almost pass as being alive. That is, if it weren't for the evidence of a bayonet wound blooming across his chest.

"Oh, sorry, sir." Syd's voice shook. "Didn't mean to bother you."

Lucely was quick to continue. "We seem to have gotten lost trying to find our parents."

"We'll just be going back this way now if you don't mind," Syd chimed in.

The soldier advanced a single pace, keeping his back to the shadows.

"*What was that I heard you birdies ch-ch-chirping on about ghosts?*"

Lucely turned around, and he was much closer to them now but still casually cleaning out his fingernails. She shifted on her feet, hands sweating, the mason jar vibrating at her waist. "Just that everyone says that this place is supposed to be super haunted, but I think it's all just a hoax to get tourists to pay for admission. Haven't seen a single ghost yet."

"*Oh, I wouldn't say* that." The man was suddenly in front of them, readying to attack, a sharpened human bone in his hand. "*Heya, ghosties, why don't we sh-sh-show them just how much of a hoax we really are?*" His mouth peeled back into a wicked smile.

Up close, Lucely could smell the death and decay radiating off him.

The girls screamed and tried to get away, but another spirit soldier now stood blocking their path—and the only way out—as more backup arrived.

The ghosts were descending from all angles now, and Lucely and Syd's hope of escaping dimmed. Lucely fought against the powerful force of the spirits holding her down, reaching for the clasp of the mason jar at her waist. Inside, Frankie charged at the glass, trying to break free to protect Lucely and Syd, but it only shuddered about as if it were sitting on top of a washing machine.

Then the latch flew open, and Frankie shot out of the jar, dealing a powerful blow to the nearest soldier and knocking him back into the confused swarm of ghosts, who released their grip on Lucely and Syd.

Lucely jumped to her feet and pointed her catcher at the grotesque-looking spirit that had rounded on them. He laughed in her face and slapped the jar out of Lucely's hands like it was nothing. She watched it crash to the floor of the room and shatter into hundreds of pieces.

"Run!" Frankie shouted in their direction. "We'll cover you!"

Lucely hadn't noticed Macarena's sudden reappearance in all the commotion. She stood back-to-back with Frankie—fists raised—looking fiercer than Lucely had ever seen her.

With a crack of her neck, Macarena shifted into a

glittering form of her human self. Light seemed to be emanating from every pore of her skin. She looked beautiful. For a moment, Lucely was transfixed, and so—it appeared—were the spirit soldiers.

"Lucely, leave it to us." Macarena met Lucely's eyes, her lips unmoving. "Once you're through the door, prop it open and wait for my signal to close it."

Hypnotized by her light, the soldiers seemed to forget about the girls and began to form a circle around Macarena and Frankie.

Lucely and Syd slipped out of the room and into the passageway just beyond the door to wait for the signal. They watched through a crack in the door, and Lucely's stomach twisted with worry.

Together, Macarena and Frankie's light grew more and more brilliant.

A moment later, the barrack exploded with a blinding light, evaporating every spirit in the room.

When the door sealed itself back into place, Lucely and Syd sank to the floor, out of breath.

"I really hope that was the signal." Syd leaned back against the wall.

"They went full-on supernova in there." Lucely shifted toward Syd's voice, arms outstretched. "But we still lost—the ghost catchers didn't work, we're no closer to figuring out the spell, and it took all of Macarena and Frankie's spirit energy just to save our pathetic butts."

Lucely fought back tears as she reached for the jar still attached to her belt—inside, the light of her fireflies blinked out.

CHAPTER ELEVEN

IT WAS OBVIOUS from their first disastrous attempt at ghost hunting that afternoon that they needed something with a much bigger punch to get rid of the evil spirits. Their homemade ghost catchers were not going to cut it. They needed *magic*.

The smooth sound of a saxophone filled the air in the Faires's house. A particularly loud note startled Syd, and she scowled. She got up and threw her bedroom door open dramatically.

"Dad, we're trying to study in here."

Her dad played a low, remorseful note by way of an apology, and Syd shook her head as she sat back down on her furry throw rug.

Lucely was sprawled out on Syd's bedroom floor playing with Syd's dog, Francisco, as they took turns reading from the giant book Babette had given them, searching for anything even remotely helpful.

While the book was filled with fascinating details about witches throughout history, they couldn't find any information about the spell they'd read or any clues as to who "E. B." was. There was nothing about hauntings and what to do about evil spirits, nor about where they might find the rest of the missing pages from the spell book.

"Where's the search-and-find function for physical books when you need it?" Lucely yawned and rolled over onto her back. Francisco copied her.

Syd flipped back to the section they'd been reading in the library and read aloud from where they'd left off.

"The Purple Coven was well-known and respected in St. Augustine and the surrounding townships, working as the village healers and doctors. However, as the hysteria of the witch trials overtook Salem, residents of St. Augustine began to look upon the coven with suspicion and fear.

"Proctor Braggs—and his wife—accused one of the young witches, Pilar, of hexing their eldest son, Michael, who had asked for her hand in marriage. The Braggs family brought Pilar to public trial and—despite vehement protests from the

betrothed—she was drowned in the San Sebastian River the very same day."

"Poor Pilar." Lucely plopped sideways onto a giant pillow.

"There's a footnote here about the book of magic that I didn't notice the other day," Syd said. *"Passed from one coven member to another, El Libro de Lobos was a written record of all the spells and knowledge Las Brujas Moradas possessed. Legend has it that after the events of Pilar's death, the coven set about creating an evil curse that would resurrect an army of the dead and open a gateway to the underworld."*

Syd stopped abruptly, eyes opened wide.

Lucely sat up with a start and looked at Syd. "Do you think . . . the spell we used was actually a *curse*? *This* curse?"

"I don't know," Syd said. "It's possible?"

Lucely fell back against the mountain of pillows on Syd's floor. "How could the coven be so reckless?! What if the curse had fallen into the wrong hands—"

"It already did, Luce . . . ours," Syd said. "There's more here though: *The only way to stop the curse is with the counter-spell from El Libro de Lobos.*"

Lucely sat up at this. "So, it's not completely hopeless?"

"I mean, technically, sure. But we just have to find a super secret coven's super secret lair and then hope that the rest of the pages will be there, including the one with the counterspell we need. It's impossible." Syd sounded defeated.

"Well, it's better than not having a solution at all," Lucely said.

"So, what's the plan, Sherlock?" Syd scratched the back of Francisco's ear, and he kicked wildly in the air.

"We search the rest of the cemeteries in town. At least now we know that the counterspell must be on one of the pages that were torn out of the book. And if we can't find them, *then* we go to Babette."

Syd bit her lip. "She's gonna kill me. 'Granny Goes Postal,' I can read the headlines now!"

"Babette might just be our only hope . . ."

Syd groaned. "Can we at least do one last mission on our own before we sentence ourselves? I want to cherish my final moments of life."

"God, you are *so* dramatic." Lucely shook her head.

"How are you gonna sneak out again with your dad watching your every move?"

"He's been pulling extra shifts for the ghost tour on weekends to try to bring in some extra money—it's always busiest leading up to Halloween. Should be easy if we go Friday night," Lucely said with more confidence than she felt. Guilt tugged at her chest, but she quickly brushed it aside. She *had* to do this, or things would only get much worse.

"My parents are going away this weekend for a jazz concert, so I'll be staying with Babette. You should ask your dad if you can sleep over! That way, once she's asleep, we can just sneak out together. But if we get caught, I'm telling them you forced me against my will."

"Traitor!"

"It's every girl for herself in the ghost-pocalypse. Sorry, not sorry!"

"Syd, if you squeal on me . . ." Lucely lunged forward and started tickling Syd. Francisco barked and rolled onto his back, wanting Lucely to give him belly rubs too.

"Stop . . . I can't . . . Luce!" Syd's face was red, and tears streamed down her cheeks.

A knock on the door interrupted what had devolved into a fit of shrieking and barking. Syd's dad popped his head in, the saxophone still hanging around his neck. "Having fun, you two?"

The girls looked at each other before breaking out into another fit of giggles.

"It's almost time for dinner, Syd. We're having your favorites: fried plantains and steak."

Syd's dad made some of the best fried plantains Lucely had ever tasted, but she would never let Simon know that. "You're welcome to stay and eat too if you'd like, Lucely."

"Oh gosh, that sounds so amazing." Lucely's mouth watered. "But I promised my dad I'd be home for dinner tonight."

"No problem. Next time! Be down in five, Syd, okay?"

Before closing the door, he shot Lucely and Syd the finger-gun move, sound effects and all. Lucely loved how weird and funny Syd's dad was. With everything going on at home lately, she missed just talking to her dad and joking around with him. Even if it was super cringeworthy.

"Tomorrow night then?" Syd raised an eyebrow.

Lucely smiled. "Tomorrow night."

CHAPTER TWELVE

EVERYTHING IN LUCELY'S HOUSE WAS ancient—the boxy television, the plastic sofa, the cream-colored PC from the nineties. Everything. But perhaps the one thing Lucely didn't mind coming from the prehistoric age were her dad's old video games.

Simon had collected every Nintendo console since he was a kid, from the Famicom to the N64, and Lucely had played every game in his collection. Among her favorite games was *Ghosts 'n Goblins*, a side-scroller where you, a knight, had to defeat various ghouls with the use of a trusty lance.

Lucely sat in the living room—legs crossed, tongue sticking out—as she tried to fight her way through the skeletons and zombies in the early stages of the nearly impossible game. But as hard as she tried, she could never get past the second level. Once again, her armor fell off, and her avatar ran across the screen in heart-printed underwear, jumping and dodging monster after monster.

"Lucely, breakfast!"

Very few things on earth could pull Lucely away from a video game. The smell of bacon, eggs, and pancakes took the first three slots on the list.

As Lucely was filling up her plate and dousing everything in a healthy bath of maple syrup, the radio on their kitchen counter perked up with an emergency weather alert:

"There continue to be reports of erratic wind patterns and flash flood–level rains all over town. Some residents have even claimed to have seen ghosts—"

Simon switched off the radio just as it was getting interesting.

"I don't know what's going on in this town anymore. If there were ghosts flying around, why haven't I seen any?" He paused and cleared his throat. "Sorry, Luce, I'm just exhausted from work."

"You can't keep staying up all night, Pa." Lucely looked down at her plate. She knew her dad was sad—maybe even depressed—about the reality that they might lose their home.

"You all packed and ready for the weekend?" Lucely's dad was a master at changing the subject.

Lucely had just scooped the last bite of scrambled eggs and pancake into her mouth, so she could only respond with a nod. She couldn't let him see how scared she was, and she couldn't admit it to herself either. If she did, all the things she knew she had to do would be even closer to impossible than they already were.

That reminded her—she hadn't said goodbye to the fireflies yet, and Babette would be pulling into their driveway any minute.

"Be right back!" she said, darting off into the backyard.

The closer Lucely got to the willow tree, the more nervous she got. The light of the cocuyos all seemed to be slightly dimmer than when she'd checked on them the night before.

Mamá's firefly wings fluttered so slightly that it was barely noticeable. To her surprise, Macarena appeared to be mostly recovered from the attack at the barrack. Lucely told her that she should keep resting, but upon hearing about Lucely and Syd's plans that evening, she insisted on coming along.

"Ayo, Manny is gonna be so jealous," Primo Benny teased, after Lucely asked him to come along too. "I'll come as long as we can get Babette to play some hip-hop in the car. No offense to Tío Simon, but I'm tired of all the bachata he's been playing lately. It's depressing, even for a dead guy."

Lucely held out a small jar for them to fly into for the car ride over before tucking it into her hoodie pocket.

"What ya doing, cuz?" Yesenia, one of Lucely's far-removed cousins, floated down from her jar to sit on the edge of the branch where Mamá's jar hung.

"Hola, Yesenia. I'm heading out for a few days, so I wanted to check in on everyone. Have you been feeling okay?"

"Mostly fine, except . . ." Yesenia zoomed close to Lucely until they were nose to nose. "Some of us have been having nightmares. Or something—I don't know what to call them exactly. But the other day, Tío Fernando climbed the tree and then jumped off, screaming the whole way down."

A shiver traced Lucely's spine. Tío Fernando had died in an airplane accident a long time ago, falling to his death when the plane malfunctioned.

"Do you think . . . the nightmares are causing you to relive your deaths?" Lucely whispered. Tía Milagros was right, and it was all making sense now. Manny crashing into the wall when he died in a car accident. Mamá had passed on in their house—one moment she was sitting in her room praying and the next she was gone. Lucely tried not to cringe; this was spooky even for her.

"Yesenia . . . how did you die?"

"I got sick." Yesenia had a far-off look on her face. "Too sick for doctors to help me."

The air began to turn ice-cold, and Lucely's breath came out in white puffs.

Yesenia's eyes opened wide, her head twitching like she was stuck on an endless, broken loop. She turned a sickly shade of gray, and not just her face but everything—her clothes, her hair, her eyes—as if she were in a black-and-white movie.

Yesenia screamed, and Lucely reached out to her, but it was too late. Her cousin was gone.

Lucely scrambled up the tree to Yesenia's mason jar. Inside, her firefly fluttered softly, her light almost out.

"No, no, no." Lucely began to cry. She had made the mistake of asking about Yesenia's death, and she'd caused her to suffer. Now Yesenia was hurt. There had to be some way to protect the fireflies while she was away.

Lucely ran into the kitchen to find the salt. Back outside, she made a large perimeter around the tree. Stepping inside the circle, she called for Tía Rosario, who appeared wearing a pink dress with tiny white flowers on it, her long hair in a sideswept braid.

"'Ción, Tía," Lucely said. "Can you keep an eye on Mamá and Yesenia?"

"Claro que si, mija." Rosario pushed her pink glasses up on the bridge of her nose. "Why is there salt everywhere?"

"I'm trying to keep whatever is giving you all nightmares—or whatever they are—away."

"Ah, yes. It has been a strange couple of days." Rosario closed her eyes and took a deep breath. "It already feels lighter. Thank you."

Lucely smiled. "I'm going to Babette's for the weekend. If anything happens . . ."

"I'll do my best to get the message to you. Don't worry." Tía Rosario held her namesake in one hand and fingered the beads worriedly.

Lucely hugged Rosario, letting herself sink into her aunt's warm embrace. "Thanks, Tía."

"Suerte y fuerza." Tía Rosario squeezed Lucely's hands tight before floating back to her jar.

Lucely inched closer to the lowest branch—the one that seemed to reach out and stroke her hair whenever she walked past the tree.

"Mamá," Lucely whispered, "I'm going to figure out a way to fix this. Don't worry, you're gonna be okay." Lucely looked up at the lights of the other fireflies around her. "You all are. I promise."

Lucely kissed two of her fingers and touched Mamá's jar, getting up to run back inside to grab her bag just as her dad called out to tell her Babette had arrived.

"Alright, Luce, now you mind Mrs. Faires this weekend. I don't want to hear even one complaint from her, understood?" Lucely's dad bent down to kiss the top of her head.

"When has anyone ever complained to you about me?" Lucely feigned shock. "Wait, don't tell me. I promise I'll be good."

"You'd better be." Simon smiled. "I know you've never seen a real flying chancleta in your time, but trust me, I can make it happen if need be."

"Don't worry, Simon. I'll keep them in line." Babette clicked her seat belt into place.

"Come onnnnn, Lucely." Syd was bouncing up and down in her seat causing the entire car to rock.

"Hey, Pa?"

Simon took a sharp breath as if Lucely had startled him. "What's up, Luce?"

"I love you. Like, a lot. And things are gonna be okay. I promise."

Her dad smiled and wiped at his eyes. He looked at Lucely with so much love that her heart felt as if it might burst. "I know you do. And I love you."

All their hope rested on the next three days. Lucely knew that if they didn't succeed this weekend, there would be nothing anyone could do. No amount of money could stop Mayor Anderson from wiping out the entire town.

That's why tonight, they wouldn't be sleeping. They'd be ghost hunting.

CHAPTER THIRTEEN

BABETTE'S CATS SAT WATCHING THEM from the wraparound porch as they pulled into the gravel driveway. Before Lucely could even thank Babette, Syd had grabbed hold of her hand and dragged her upstairs to the loft bedroom where they'd be staying.

"I've been dying to show you something. I was searching through my grandma's stuff downstairs, and look." Syd pulled a candle out from her backpack. It was white with red flames painted on the side and some sort of symbol wrapping its way around the wax.

"What is it for?" asked Lucely, inspecting the candle.

"It's a protection candle," Syd whispered. "Supposedly it is meant to invoke the God of War."

"That sounds dangerous."

"If we come up against the library monsters again, it will be, for them. But the candle is supposed to work for whoever lights it, and it's gotta be super powerful because I found it in my grandma's hidden safe."

"What? How'd you get inside? And what if she notices? We'll be toast."

"If she figures out we're sneaking out tonight, we'll be toast anyway. Might as well not die at the hands of a mega ghost."

Lucely nodded in agreement. Syd had a good point. Besides, they knew now what they were up against, and they couldn't exactly stroll into the next cemetery with no way of defending themselves.

"What's the plan, then?" Syd stuffed the candle back into her bag.

"We're going to check out Huguenot Cemetery tonight. According to my dad, it's one of the most haunted. And there's a church, which adds to the creep factor. I have our routes mapped out with all the mausoleums marked on my phone *and* on a printed map just in case we run out of battery."

"Routes? *Plural?*" Syd's eyes widened.

"Well . . . you're *not* gonna like this, but I think we should split up . . ." Lucely cringed.

"Splitting up is the last thing we should do! But hey"—Syd held her hands up—"you're the boss. If I die, please be kind to my ghost. Let me live in your tree or something."

"Do you think we should bring Chunk?" Lucely picked the fat cat up and nuzzled her nose.

"Meow," responded Chunk.

"You think she'll be quiet when we sneak out?" Lucely asked.

"She'll yell louder if we don't take her with us. She's so nosey, I swear."

"We should bring some of those treats she likes just in case."

"One question though: If we do find one of the missing pages from the book, then what?"

"*Then* we recite the spell. The sooner, the better. The fireflies are getting sicker every day, and the town is being overrun with spirits." Lucely sighed. "And if we don't find a new place to live soon—or find a way to save the house—I guess we'll just be on the street."

"We won't let that happen." Syd threw herself on top of Lucely and hugged her. "I'd tell my parents to let you stay with us. Or here with Babette. You can sleep with Chunk in her bed."

Lucely giggled, melting into Syd's arms.

"If we can fix it by Halloween, do you think there's a chance you could stay?"

"Maybe?" Lucely got up on her elbows and turned to face Syd. "Last year on Halloween I remember Dad saying we made over five thousand dollars. That's nowhere near what we need, but maybe if we make that much, it'll be enough to convince Mr. Vincent to let us keep the house a little while longer. And who knows—once the real ghosts are gone, maybe tourists will be curious enough to come and see what the deal is."

"Let's work on that tomorrow. Tonight, we focus on finding the next clue," Syd said.

For the first time since this whole thing started, Lucely had some hope, even if it was only a glimmer.

There was a sharp knock on the front door that startled Lucely out of her reading. They had been in Babette's library—with her permission this time—supposedly reading up on ghosts but in fact trying to find more information on the counterspell. The library sat near the front of the house, and both Lucely and Syd snuck up to the archway between the library and the foyer to eavesdrop just outside Babette's view. Lucely listened as Babette opened the door and a familiar voice greeted her.

"Mayor Anderson, this is a surprise," Babette said. "What are you doing out visiting residents so late? You usually send that much smarter assistant of yours around."

"It's nice to see you too, Babette."

Syd and Lucely looked at each other. What was Mayor Anderson doing there?

Lucely chanced a peek and could see the ridiculously tall man towering over Babette in the doorway. He tugged on his white handlebar mustache and then smoothed his long trench coat over his chest before handing something to Babette.

"As you know, the annual Halloween Festival is coming up soon, so I thought I'd do a bit of local canvassing, passing out fliers and such. It would be a great pleasure if you could join us for our little soiree."

Babette looked at the flyer and crumpled it up. Mayor Anderson's gaze shifted to where Lucely and Syd were hiding, his mouth spreading into an unnatural smile as if his face were made of putty. His eyes flashed a sickly green as he turned back to Babette.

Lucely's hand flew to Syd's mouth just in time to stifle the gasp she knew was coming. They both stood there, frozen in fear.

"I'm not interested." Babette moved to close the door, but the mayor stopped her with one long arm.

"I think it would be advisable for you to at least consider—"

"I think it would be *advisable* for you to get off my property before I call the police. Or I can hex you." Babette did not mess around.

The mayor held up two hands in surrender. "Have a pleasant evening, Babette. We hope you will reconsider."

And with that the mayor left.

Babette slammed the door and whipped around faster than Lucely and Syd could pull back from their hiding spot.

"I think it's about time for bed for you two little eavesdroppers."

The girls waited until Babette had gone into her room and shut the door before going over their supplies. Chunk, Data, and Sloth had parked themselves on the girls' bags and were watching them with casual disinterest.

"When I said be prepared, I meant to go *ghost hunting*, not for a weekend trip to Disney," Lucely said.

"You said be ready, which means I bring all my ghost stuff. You know I'm like this. Accept me or lose my friendship." Syd crossed her arms.

"You're so extra." Lucely laughed. "Okay, what's in the bag?"

"So this is a protection amulet to help ward off evil spirits, all the way from New Orleans. And this is a fresh ghost catcher." Syd held up a spray-painted mason jar. "I made it myself and took my time this go around, so hopefully it actually does something, unlike the first one. It might not work as well as Babette's stuff, but it should do the trick. Did you bring the fireflies?"

Lucely nodded and put one hand on the skinny container holding her cousins Macarena and Benny. They were some of the youngest and strongest fireflies, plus she didn't know if she could handle Tía Milagros *and* evil spirits all at once.

"Cool. We're gonna put them into the mason jars, and they should help attract evil spirits." Syd reached for the jar.

"Hold up." Lucely held one hand up to stop Syd. "Two things: One, you promised they wouldn't get hurt. And trapping them with evil spirits doesn't sound very cozy or safe. Two, I still don't know how a spray-painted mason jar is supposed to work against an ancient spell? It doesn't look nearly as cool as the Muon Traps they use in *Ghostbusters*."

"We're not in *Ghostbusters*. This is real life. And my DIY ghost catchers are better than nothing. I had the formula all wrong last time; it's all in the *black* paint."

"You know what? You're right. Maybe after we save the town from vicious spirits dragging us all into the underworld, you can sell your handcrafted hippie ghost catchers on Etsy.

Name your store Sassy Syd's!" Lucely couldn't hold back the laugh that fought its way out of her.

Syd narrowed her eyes at Lucely, but a smirk played on her lips. "Anyway, I brought three more protection amulets, gifts from Babette on my birthdays. We should all wear one. Even Chunk. Also, *Sassy Syd's* has a nice ring to it, and I'm putting that in my journal."

Syd handed Lucely a necklace with a giant sapphire pendant in the center. Syd's had a beautiful amethyst stone, and Chunk's was made from a clear crystal. They each slipped an amulet on, and Lucely felt a warmth spread throughout her body. These things must have been *strong*.

Chunk mewed in protest when Syd tied it around her neck, trying to swat at it with her paws. Once she'd calmed down, Syd put Chunk back on top of her bag, and the cat began snoring in seconds.

"I picked up some Florida water too, which helps ward off bad energy and evil spirits. And these stones are supposed to ward off demons and possession."

"Oh gosh, I need one of those." Lucely held her hand out, remembering how awful it felt for Mamá's ghost to go through her. Syd dropped the pink stone in her hand—it was cold and smooth. "You sure this is going to work?"

"Well, I've never been possessed, but you have so stop trying to drag my tools. I made a ghost catcher for you too." Syd gave Lucely an identical black mason jar with a wire handle and a lid that flipped open with the flick of your finger and closed with a clasp.

Lucely inspected the jar; it had a small, clear compartment inside that was closed off from an open area around it. "Do my fireflies go in the middle?" she asked.

"Yep, and the evil ghosts go on the outside. They'll be safe, I promise. I washed all these in Florida water, and the ugly ghosts are gonna be useless once we trap them inside."

Lucely bit her lip and nodded reluctantly. She really hoped Syd was right.

"I also brought *El Libro de Lobos*, just in case we find something. Two flashlights, a banana, some candles, a loaf of bread, some cash, and a fake mustache."

"I'm not even gonna ask." Lucely shook her head.

"Hey, we don't know if we're gonna get abducted or lost, but we're definitely going to get hungry. And the mustache is a disguise in case we run into Mayor Creepy again and he spots us. I only have one though."

"You can use it," Lucely said, laughing.

"Alright, but don't come begging me for my 'stache if we get caught."

Around ten o'clock, Babette fell into a deep, snoring sleep, just as Syd had predicted. By ten thirty, the girls, along with Chunk, were already riding toward the cemetery.

They rode their bikes through the foggy night, the occasional specter rising from the tree-lined streets. Chunk sat in a basket at the front of Syd's bike, swaddled in a blanket to keep warm.

"What do you think the mayor wanted with Babette?" Lucely asked Syd as they rode.

"Nothing good. That's for sure."

Once they'd reached the entrance to Huguenot Cemetery, Lucely and Syd hid their bikes behind a giant elm.

"I drew up a map of all the mausoleums in the cemetery. Some of them will be locked and some will be open, but I got this"—Lucely patted the crowbar sticking out of her backpack—"in case we have to muscle our way in."

Syd clapped softly, and Chunk hissed, startled awake from a nap.

"There are twelve mausoleums in this cemetery. You sure you don't want to split up—"

Syd cut Lucely off with a raised hand. "Have you never seen a horror movie, ever? *Scooby Doo*? Besides, I'm scared, girl! We're going together."

"Fine, *chicken*. We could've covered more ground separately, but if you're too scared . . ." Lucely teased.

"And if the evil spirits come for one of us, hmm? Then

what? I am *not* about to die alone. No, ma'am," Syd said, a hint of fear flashing through her before she broke into a nervous laugh.

"Just follow me, Syd. I memorized the maps."

The iron fences of Huguenot Cemetery were rusted over and shot ten feet into the night sky. As Syd looked up at the fence, Lucely held the padlock keeping the doors shut in her hand.

She gave the lock a few good whacks with her crowbar, but it didn't even budge.

"This is not just locked, it's super locked. And unless you can magic up some sort of Alohomora spell, there's no way we're getting in." Lucely shook her head.

"You give up too easily, Luna," Syd teased. She gestured for Lucely to follow her, and together they walked their bikes to the other side of the cemetery.

"Here." Syd put her bike down and pointed to a patch of dirt beneath a chain-link fence. The ground dipped right under the fence and left almost enough space for them both to get through.

"We can dig a bit so there's enough room for us to squeeze under," suggested Syd.

"How'd you even know this was here?" Lucely laughed.

"I scouted the place before. Honestly, what kind of amateur ghost hunter do you think I am?"

"Uh, I'm pretty sure this is only your second 'ghost hunt,' Syd."

"Technically yes, but I've watched and planned enough of them that it doesn't *feel* like my first one." Syd dropped down and started digging as Lucely joined her.

"This is gross. There are probably, like, dead people worms in here." Lucely made a face.

"Oh my gosh, why would you say that right now?"

The girls laughed and kept digging with their hands until enough dirt had been pushed out of the way for them to fit under the fence.

"I'll go first, you pass me Chunk, and then you go, okay?" Lucely said, and Syd nodded in response.

Lucely pressed her body as far down as she could go and shimmied beneath the fence. It smelled like fresh soil, and Lucely hoped her clothes weren't getting completely ruined. Once on the other side, she wiped her jeans down as much as possible while Syd coaxed Chunk to crawl under the fence.

"Come on, Chunk, get your big butt over there." Syd nudged the cat gently, but she wouldn't move.

Chunk let out one long meow in protest, and Lucely dropped to her knees, holding a piece of string cheese out and making cooing noises.

Chunk bolted straight under the fence.

"It's always food with you," Syd said, before slipping under the fence herself.

"Good thing I brought string cheese," said Lucely.

"Good thing my grandma's cats are solely motivated by food."

The cemetery seemed darker than the rest of the world somehow. And colder. The trees swayed, and Lucely tried her best not to look at them. In the dark, they looked like ghosts dancing.

Chunk sat alert in a baby sling wrapped around Syd's chest. As they walked through the misty graveyard, Chunk began whining softly, and Syd whispered comforting words. She was quiet for a moment but whimpered again as they approached the mausoleum.

"She okay?" asked Lucely.

"She shouldn't have to use the bathroom; she went before we got here. She can probably sense the ghosts."

Lucely rubbed the cat's head, and Chunk licked her before hiding her head inside the pouch, shivering.

"Come on." Lucely tried to ignore her nerves as she pushed open the heavy marble door.

The mausoleum was even colder than the cemetery. They shone their flashlights inside, casting long shadows across the walls and floor. They stood so close, Lucely could feel the goose bumps on Syd's leg up against hers. Chunk was crying frantically now.

"Maybe you should stay outside with her to keep watch," Lucely said. "I don't want her tiny heart to burst."

"No way I'm standing out there alone." Syd pulled something from her pocket and gave it to the cat. Lucely could hear Chunk chewing happily, and the whimpering subsided.

They inspected the right side of the tomb together, Syd's hand gripping Lucely's arm so hard it hurt. "You gonna be okay? You usually love this stuff," Lucely said.

"I know, but I'm freaked out. Chunk is scared, and she's hardly ever scared. I just have the heebie-jeebies."

"We're in a graveyard in the middle of the night; it would be weird of you *not* to have the heebie-jeebies," Lucely said. "I'm just trying to keep my cool because we have at least another four hours of this to go before we have to head back home."

"Right." Syd straightened up and let go of Lucely.

They inspected the other side of the tomb and were back at the entrance a few moments later.

"Nothing." Lucely ruffled her curls in frustration.

"Come on, next one is about twenty paces to our left. No sense in messing up your hair."

The next mausoleum was much bigger than the first, with

two corridors leading to separate rooms. They stuck together, not wanting to lose sight of each other.

Lucely ran her hands along the dusty walls and looked for hidden nooks and traps. Syd shone her flashlight inside the coffin and felt around with a long stick.

"No luck," said Lucely after they'd searched the entire tomb.

Loud squeaks came from every corner of the next mausoleum. The flash of a long tail or musty gray fur scurrying across the ground made Lucely cringe, and she tried not to scream. But aside from the giant rats that lurked in its shadows, the tomb was empty. So were the next three. It was one in the morning by the time they reached the seventh mausoleum, and Lucely was beginning to worry they'd never find the missing pages.

Syd shivered. Despite the normally mild weather, both girls had succumbed to a cold in their bones that they couldn't seem to shake no matter how much they jumped around or rubbed their limbs. A light drizzle came down and made pockets of gray light in the mist.

They made their way into one of the largest mausoleums in the cemetery. It was so cold that goose bumps covered Lucely's body and her nose felt like that one time they'd spent Christmas in New York years ago.

Every time it got unnaturally cold, something bad happened. With Mamá and Manny, and at the fort. Lucely shivered and pushed that thought out of her head. The mausoleum smelled like mothballs and wet clothing and the plastic of old toys abandoned in a secondhand store. Just as she thought of the toys, Lucely heard what sounded like a small child laughing and feet scuttling across the cement ground. She stopped and swirled around at the noise, but there was nothing there. Only darkness.

"Something doesn't feel right." Lucely moved slowly toward the entrance of the mausoleum.

Lucely opened the door, and Chunk howled so loudly it didn't seem like it could have come from her. And then the door slammed shut. In the same instant, Lucely dropped her flashlight, and its light went out with a painful crack. Lucely put both hands on the handle and pulled, but the door refused to open.

"What's happening?" Syd yelled.

"Help me! The door is stuck."

They both pulled on the handle, but it wouldn't budge. They shook, kicked, and screamed, but nothing worked. Then something moved behind them. Both girls stood stock-still. They heard a creak again, and then there was a blast of air so cold the hairs on Lucely's arms stood on end.

"Who's there?" Lucely asked without looking back.

She reached slowly toward the door again, but the blast of cold air overtook her, and they both screamed. Chunk joined them with a howl.

Somebody mumbled in the darkness, their words sounding almost like . . . a song. But the voice was inhuman, low, gravely, and menacing like the growl of a jaguar.

"I've caught two little flies in my web, in my web. Two little flies, they disturbed me now they're dead."

Syd's flashlight began to blink on and off in tune with the song before plunging them into complete darkness with whatever was in there with them. The voice laughed maniacally and Lucely thought she might pass out from fear.

"We're sorry." Syd's voice trembled. "We were only trying to help you go home." She slowly turned her backpack toward Lucely, who nodded. Syd laughed nervously but kept talking. "We're just two kids. Not sure what we're doing really. We thought we'd be able to help you, but you obviously don't need our help."

Lucely started to take the bottle of Florida water out, but Syd shook her head. Instead, Lucely pulled out a cylinder from the bag; a giant piece of tape on it read *salt* in Syd's bubbly handwriting. From the corner of her eye, Lucely saw Syd nod ever so slightly, and she handed the salt over to her friend.

"We're just gonna make our way out of here now. Thanks for your kind hospitality." Syd raised the container over her head and spun it in a circle throwing salt everywhere.

The creature screeched, the sound like nails on a chalkboard above them, and Lucely looked up. It was another mist monster. It had gathered above them and was swooping down again, coming right at her.

Chunk had gotten free of her baby sling somehow and was now cowering behind Syd's leg.

The mist swept toward them again. They screamed, and Chunk jumped into Lucely's arms. Lucely shut her eyes tight, her father's face flashing in her mind's eye. If she got hurt tonight, would she ever see him again?

Syd made another circle with salt, but this time, as the mist came barreling toward them, they ran. The creature crashed into the salt circle and cried out in pain, barely missing the girls. In the same instant, the door creaked open, bringing a gust of wind into the mausoleum and getting salt everywhere.

Lucely and Syd bolted through the door and into the night.

Brambles scratched Lucely's legs as she tried to keep a straight path in the dark. Chunk mewed and hissed in her arms as they ran.

"She's . . . so . . . heavy," panted Lucely.

"Don't call her Chunk for nothin'," Syd said.

They scrambled under the fence, and Lucely tried not to think of worms and dead things. When they reached their bikes, Lucely deposited Chunk into Syd's basket and hopped on her own bike. Just as they began to peddle away, Lucely turned to see the monster standing in the marble doorway of the mausoleum, the moonlight revealing a form they hadn't seen before.

Its vacant eyes were staring directly at Lucely and Syd, and aside from the gray skin and black hole of a mouth, it looked exactly like Mayor Anderson.

CHAPTER FOURTEEN

THE GHOULISH MIST MAYOR stalked toward them, growing in size with each step. A cloud of dirt and bramble swirled around it like a powerful tornado, obscuring its human form completely. Mayor Anderson had become a roiling, shapeless, terrifying *thing*. It was like many spirits had conjoined; multiple sets of eyes glowed above mouths that howled in unison. Thick green veins pulsed over every inch of its putrid mass.

"Oh my gosh, oh my gosh, oh my gosh. Go, go, go, Syd!" Lucely pedaled faster than she ever had in her life. Chunk hissed loudly from behind her as the tires of Syd's bike crunched through the dead leaves beneath the elm tree.

"*Ahhhhhhhhhhhh.*"

The mist monster blasted a wall of frigid air toward them, causing Lucely's limbs to stiffen. Pedaling became harder and harder until she was going so slowly that she was nearly at a standstill. Beside her, Syd was in the same predicament.

"What do we do?" Syd looked behind them; the mist monster couldn't have been more than a hundred yards away and was gaining fast.

"The salt, the Florida water, all of it. Let's use all of it. We can't outrun it, so we have to try to fight it."

"Are you for real? That thing's gonna swallow us whole!"

"Syd, neither of us can even pedal, Chunk is gonna die of a heart attack, and you want to argue? Trust me!"

Syd shook her head but got off her bike, taking out the rest of her ghost stuff.

Lucely grabbed the salt that sat in the basket with Chunk and made a giant circle around them.

"Stay here, baby girl," she whispered to Chunk.

Syd was lighting candles and putting them in as many places just outside the circle as she could. Each of them had a different saint depicted on it in jewel-tone paint.

Lucely handed Syd the Florida water, and Syd dabbed some on her finger before making the sign of the cross on each of their foreheads. They ran back over to splash some on Chunk too.

The howling was getting closer, and the girls stood in the circle, one ghost catcher in each of their hands, the faint twinkle of Macarena's and Benny's lights within.

"I really hope this works," Lucely said, reaching out for Syd's free hand.

"Me too."

"Meow," added Chunk.

Syd grabbed Lucely's hand. Together, they stood—ghost catchers up and open—facing the oncoming mist monster.

A howling noise pierced the ink-black night, and Syd's hand shook in Lucely's.

Lucely looked at her friend and nodded, squeezing her hand. *I'm here*, she thought but could not say out loud, her fear keeping her words trapped in her throat. But Syd seemed to understand, and a look of determination replaced the terror in her eyes.

The air around them became frigid; Lucely's breath came out in tiny marshmallow-like puffs. She wished more than anything that her fireflies would be okay. Now that they'd been this far from the tree for so long, she wasn't sure they'd even have the energy to help.

She closed her eyes just for a moment and imagined her fireflies surrounding her and Syd, creating an impenetrable ball of light to protect them.

The creature was before them now—taller than even the biggest tree in the cemetery—and it took every bit of Lucely's self-control not to run.

"Don't leave the circle," said Syd through clenched teeth. "It's our best chance."

Just as the words left her lips, the mist monster swooped down, shrieking as it barreled toward them, its howls mixing with the screams coming from Lucely, Syd, and Chunk.

And just as fast as it had come at them, it was past them. Both girls looked back in unison and then at each other. The creature rounded back, but just before it reached the circle, it was split in two, as if the protection circle had cut it in half. Its scream was bloodcurdling, but still it was no closer to penetrating the circle.

Chunk had escaped her basket and was now hissing at the monster, puffing up her fur to make herself bigger.

The mist monster flew up so high Lucely could barely see it. Then with one terrible scream, it dove straight down at them.

Lucely screamed and held on to Syd with her eyes closed, too terrified to do anything but stand there. Again, the mist monster could not enter their circle. It opened its hideous mouth, thick green veins flashing as if there were lightning within the monster, and roared like a lion as close to their faces as it could get. The smell alone was enough to knock out an entire soccer team. Then it turned with the force of a tornado and headed back in the direction of the mausoleum.

An eerie quiet blanketed the graveyard. Lucely's eyes remained half shut until a soft mew from Chunk gave her the courage to pop just one eye open. Syd was still holding on to her for dear life.

"Syd, I think it's gone," she whispered.

Syd opened her eyes and looked around. They were alone in the pitch-black night.

Everything in Lucely's body told her to run, to go home, but if that monster attacked them, it was for a reason. Maybe it was protecting something here on these grounds.

"Should we check out the church next?" Syd asked, reading Lucely's mind.

She nodded in response, still too shaken up to say much.

They walked in silence toward the church. Even Chunk was quiet; the only sound was the night air whooshing softly and the occasional crunch of gravel or twigs underfoot. Lucely's stomach tightened with anxiety when someone cleared their throat just next to her ear.

"Ah!" Lucely jumped back and spun around toward the noise.

Standing there in the dark was a man. He was wearing a fancy suit that didn't look like anything from this century and holding a hat to his chest.

"Excuse me, miss, sorry to have frightened you. Have you seen my teeth?" The man—or ghost rather—smiled and showed them he was missing several teeth.

Lucely grabbed Syd's hand and turned to run, but the ghost simply swooped in front of them with a distressed look on his face.

"It's quite rude to walk away when someone asks you a question, dear. I only require assistance with my missing teeth. My name is Judge John Stickney, 1882. Pleased to meet you."

"Uh, I'm Lucely, and that's Syd." Lucely figured that if this ghost meant to hurt them, he already would have. And she didn't get the strange, awful, cold feeling she did with the mist monster. He was more like her fireflies. Dead but just slightly see-through. "Is 1882 when you were born?"

"Oh no, that's when I died." A stricken look crossed the judge's face. "And those terrible thieves stole my gold teeth! You haven't happened to see them, have you?"

He was so hopeful and seemed so earnest, Lucely actually felt bad she didn't know where this guy's missing teeth were.

Syd threw her hands up and shrugged. "Sorry, Judge John, we have no idea where your teeth are."

"We can keep an eye out for them though," Lucely offered.

"That would be most wonderful." The judge clapped two translucent hands together. "It's more than anyone else has ever offered. Usually people just scream and run away from me. I can't imagine why."

"Yeah, it's a mystery to all of us," Lucely said.

"I'll be off now, but do remember to give word if you find my teeth. It's awfully hard to be respectable without them, and I have a party to attend with the Pancake sisters."

"Pancake sisters?" asked Syd.

"Yes, an unusual name, but what can one really expect from witches?" the judge said, laughing. "So long, Syd and Lucely. I hope to see you soon and that you bring news of my teeth."

With that, Judge John floated up and away from them, disappearing between the trees.

"That was about a thirteen on a one-to-ten scale of weirdness," said Lucely.

"I was gonna say ten, but thirteen sounds more accurate."

"At least he didn't try to kill us."

"Or take *our* teeth," said Syd.

Thunder rumbled overhead. As they walked on, a flash of lightning illuminated the sky. Then came the rain, drenching them immediately. They tucked their heads down and ran, water and mud splashing underfoot. However, the closer they seemed to get to the church, the farther it seemed to move away from them. Lucely let out a sigh of frustration, and her breath came out in a white puffy cloud. They looked at each other when Lucely noticed something else.

"Where's Chunk?"

"I thought she was with you." Syd's voice was laced with alarm.

Lucely shook her head, and her heart sank thinking of Chunk being lost and alone in the cemetery.

"Oh my gosh." Syd started running around and calling for Chunk, and Lucely did the same.

"Chunk!" They cried, but the wind and the rain made everything harder to hear and see.

Lucely saw Syd's shoulders slump. The cemetery was so dark, and she could've been hiding anywhere. Lucely pulled Syd under the protection of a giant elm. Under its branches and leaves, the wind was a little calmer.

"Poor Chunk. I can't believe we lost her." Syd put her hands on her head.

"We'll find her. Don't worry."

Just then, Lucely saw a flash of white streak behind the church.

"Come on." She pulled Syd in the direction of the church, hoping it was the light of the moon reflecting on Chunk's cat eyes.

CHAPTER FIFTEEN

WHEN SHE WAS TEN, Lucely had watched a scary movie that, looking back, wasn't very scary at all. Still, she'd had nightmares for a week. Every night, the monster from the movie would come to her in her sleep—jagged teeth gleaming, eyes red, horrible black claws. It wasn't until Mamá said a protection prayer over her and instructed her to cross her slippers in front of her bed at night that the nightmares stopped. However, Lucely would've gladly traded her nightmare monster for whatever was staring down at them now.

Everything about this creature was terrifying. Its gargantuan mass was covered in scales, like a dragon, except the scales were see-through, and its eyes glowed green and red.

The spirit seemed to be searching for something—for them?—exhaling streams of white-hot flames into the air and setting the trees around them ablaze.

Lucely grabbed Syd's hand and sprinted toward the church.

"Oh gosh, oh gosh, oh gosh, we're gonna die!" Syd screamed as they ran.

"Don't talk like that! 'Goonies never say die.' Remember?" Lucely tried one of the doors of the church, but it was locked.

"Come on!" Lucely said as they searched for another entrance. The ground trembled beneath them, and the sight of the dragon spirit on their heels sent a fresh wave of terror through Lucely.

Streams of fire licked the ground around them as Lucely tried another door. This one wasn't locked, but it was heavy.

Syd and Lucely each grabbed on to one of the handles and pulled as hard as they could.

"RAAAAAAAAAAA!"

The monster was on their side of the cathedral now and closing in on them. It shot a stream of fire in their direction, singeing the end of Lucely's sweatshirt.

"Pull, Syd! As hard as you can on three!"

Syd nodded frantically, sweat flying from her face as she did.

"One, two, three!" Lucely yelled.

Just as the dragon opened its mouth and took aim at them again, the door groaned open enough that they were able to slip inside. Lucely slammed the heavy door shut and jammed the thick metal lock into place.

They crouched beneath one of the pews toward the back of the cathedral, trying to steady their breathing.

"What are we gonna do now?" Syd whispered, wiping tears and sweat from her eyes.

"I don't think that dragon thing can get in here," said Lucely. "But we should be ready in case."

As quickly as they could, Lucely and Syd began making a safety circle around themselves. Once their salt circle was complete, they started lighting as many candles as they could before the monster got too close.

The entrance to the church rattled violently; the dragon spirit seemed to be ramming against the doors repeatedly, causing them to splinter. Howls of rage erupted from the other side.

"It's gonna eat us," Syd said. "It was nice knowing you, Luce."

"We're not gonna die. Not tonight, not like this," Lucely said, with more conviction than she felt. She wouldn't let Syd feel afraid if she could help it. She could do that, at least.

Syd nodded in her direction and took the ghost catchers out of her bag, handing one to Lucely and holding hers open.

"Put your catcher down right outside the circle," Syd said.

"What about Macarena and Benny?" Lucely asked. She had been so busy being scared out of her mind that she had forgotten all about them. She didn't think any of her firefly family had been away from the tree for so long, and her heart lurched at the thought of them being hurt.

"We're okay." Macarena's voice floated toward Lucely.

"This is more fun than I've had in twenty years!" Benny's voice came from his catcher.

"Maybe the Florida water will keep them safe too?" suggested Syd.

"I hope so," Lucely said. "Okay, so what are *we* gonna do if it doesn't work?"

"Hide. Or run. Anything but stand here and get turned into barbecue."

"*RAAAAAAAAAAA!*"

The monster's shriek reverberated throughout the church from behind them, its head now halfway through the splintered doors. Flames erupted from its open mouth, setting a few pews on fire.

They broke into a run, narrowly missing the monster's attack and leaving their catchers behind. Lucely and Syd stood with their backs against the wall of the church, with the dragon across the room from them and the ghost catchers and circle of salt at the center. There was no exit in sight.

"We need to try to get the catchers," Lucely said.

"Are you serious? That thing has its head halfway inside. One more push and we're dino snacks!"

"We can either get the catchers and *maybe* stand a chance, or be totally helpless and get eaten once it finds us hiding back here. Plus, we can't leave the fireflies." Lucely looked over at Syd.

"Fine, but we go together," said Syd.

Lucely smiled at Syd, and they held hands again.

"This dragon's gonna wish it had never messed with Lucely Luna and Syd Faires!"

The far side of the cathedral erupted in a hail of wood and stone. Most of the dragon's head was now peeking through the church's splintered door, smoke billowing from its massive nostrils.

The dragon roared just as Lucely and Syd attempted to sneak past the organ, startling them both backward and onto the organ's massive keys. The pipes blared out a loud, disjointed note, catching the dragon's attention. It turned on them and let out a violent jet of flames.

"Duck!" Lucely shouted, and they both dove for the floor, narrowly escaping the fire.

"No more loud noises, got it," whispered Syd.

Finally, the girls reached the pew nearest to the salt circle and the ghost catchers.

With one final squeeze of her hand, Lucely took off, Syd at her side.

Just as they reached the circle, the dragon broke through the door and charged right for them.

There was no time for Lucely to react, no time to turn back, no time to even look at Syd.

Lucely closed her eyes and threw her arms up in self-defense, ghost catcher in hand.

Then a warm light rushed past her.

"Back, foul beast!" a familiar voice commanded.

Lucely opened her eyes to see Babette standing between them and the dragon, a wand held up to the creature's snout. The dragon scuttled back, sneering at them. It took one tentative step forward, looking scared for once.

"One more step, and I'll turn you into a rain cloud, you oversize iguana," Babette spat.

As if to challenge her, the dragon moved to advance.

Babette made a circle with her wand, and a wave of purple light pulsed out at the monster. It bayed, throwing its massive head back and attacking them with another rain of fire. But this time, they had Babette. She rushed at the dragon, wand up, her dreadlocks flying behind her. Her cape curled at the end like a barrier, keeping Lucely and Syd safe.

"*Reverse, rearward from whence you came!*" Babette's voice boomed as if it were coming from all around them. The organ began to play in tune with her voice.

The dragon shrieked and scrambled back, trying to escape Babette.

"*Back, back! Into the flames!*" Violet flames shot from her wand and hit the dragon directly between the eyes. It let out one final, bloodcurdling shriek, and then it began to burn.

"Uh, best if you don't see what happens next," said Babette, turning around to face them.

When the dragon roared again, so loudly this time that the stained-glass windows shattered in a hail of rainbow shards, Babette threw her large purple cape over the girls, plunging them into darkness.

CHAPTER SIXTEEN

BABETTE LOOMED over Lucely and Syd, pacing back and forth in a silent rage as they sat petrified in her living room. If they weren't already dead, they would be soon.

The good news was that Chunk wasn't lost. She was sitting on Babette's desk looking every bit as disappointed as Syd's grandmother.

Every few minutes, Babette would stop pacing, look at the girls, and shake her head. Or she'd stop, look at the girls, open her mouth as if to start yelling, and then continue to pace without saying a word. Lucely was pretty sure this was a form of torture.

"Now, I'm gonna ask you both once, and I expect the truth, or I will go straight to your parents." Babette finally stopped pacing and dropped her arms to her sides, a look of bewilderment on her face. "What were you two doing in that cemetery in the middle of the night?"

She stood there, waiting, while Syd and Lucely exchanged looks.

"Babette, we promise we were only trying to help." Lucely held her hands up.

"How did you know where we were?" Syd gave her grandmother a suspicious look.

Chunk mewed.

"Chunk?" Syd asked.

"There's a lot you don't know about this town. And about me. But I am the one asking *you* questions right now, young lady. And unless you want to be turned into something unpleasant, I suggest you start talking."

Syd gulped. "Toads," she whispered into Lucely's ear.

"Okay, okay, Babette. I will explain everything. It's mostly my fault," Lucely started.

"I helped," said Syd proudly.

Babette shot her a look, and Syd cringed.

"It started because of . . ." Lucely's voice shook. She'd never told anyone but Syd about her fireflies. But it wasn't like she could lie to Babette now. "My grandmother got sick. I mean, she's . . . It's complicated."

Lucely took a deep breath, trying to settle her nerves.

"Oh, baby, I'm sorry." Babette's face softened. She knelt at Lucely's level, her warm hands supporting Lucely's elbows.

"I just wanted to help, and then our history teacher told us about Las Brujas Moradas and their spell book," Lucely continued. "And I thought there might be something in that book that could help Mamá. This might sound weird, Babette, but I can see ghosts. Real ones, in my house. They live as firefl—"

"You think I don't know?" Babette crossed her arms in front of her chest with a smile. "Who do you think babysat your father when he was your age?"

This caught Lucely off guard, but it was Syd who spoke up first. "What, really?! I didn't think you were that—"

"I'd hold my tongue if I were you, Sydney Faires." Babette's eyes narrowed at her. "Now, Lucely, what were you saying about your fireflies?"

"It's just . . . lately they've all been getting sick and acting strange. So when we read about *El Libro de Lobos* in that history book you lent us, we hoped that—by finding the missing pages that had been torn out—we might find a spell that would help revive the fireflies before they faded away forever."

Syd reached over and squeezed Lucely's hand. "Nothing happened when we first recited the spell we found. But then all the hauntings started happening around St. Augustine."

"You girls recited a spell from *The Book of Wolves* without knowing what it was intended for? Of all the—" Babette stood and started pacing again. "We'll skip over the detail of *how* you came to obtain my book without my knowledge for now, but—be assured—Babette never forgets. Now, do you recall the name of the spell you recited?"

Both girls looked down.

"I think it was called A Spell to Wake the Sleeping." Syd sounded like a cornered mouse. "We have the paper here."

Syd produced the spell book from her backpack and offered it to her grandmother.

Babette flipped it open to the torn-out section and found the folded-up spell tucked into the spine. Her face blanched as she looked it over. She quickly folded the paper and shut the book.

"Well, I'm certainly not happy that you betrayed my trust—you know you're not allowed to take my things out of this house without my permission—but I'm glad you're safe. You two are lucky to be alive. Though that *does* complicate things."

"Us being alive?" Syd's eyes grew to twice their size.

"No no no." Babette stood up. "The spell you cast. And the fact that *you* cast it means that *only you* can undo it."

"Is there anything we can do, Grandma?"

Babette was silent for a moment. "You girls should've come to me first. You know you can trust me—especially you, Syd. Nevertheless, there's nothing to do now but find that counterspell and try to fix this. And I'm going to help you."

Babette smiled and clapped her hands together.

"But first, I'm going to teach you how to catch a ghost."

CHAPTER SEVENTEEN

ACCORDING TO BABETTE, there were four basic rules to ghost hunting:

1. Be prepared.
2. Don't go alone.
3. Respect the dead.
4. Always have a cat.

Babette made Syd and Lucely repeat these four rules so many times that Lucely was sure she'd never forget them as long as she lived.

"What in the world is this?" Babette dangled one of Syd's homemade ghost catchers from one elegant finger, as if it were filled with cat poop.

"It's a ghost catcher," said Syd.

"A what? Child, this is nothing but a mason jar painted black." Babette quirked an eyebrow before walking to the back of the shop. "I've got the real thing. Follow me."

Babette pulled a book on the shelf, and the secret doorway opened.

Lucely and Syd followed her into a dark room, and Babette tugged on a chain above her head. Instead of a lightbulb though, a series of candles throughout the room began to light themselves.

"Cool," Lucely and Syd whispered to each other.

The room felt like a sacred place, not the sort of place to yell or speak too loudly. But it felt no less creepy than it had when they'd entered the first time with just their phone flashlights. In fact, it was creepier. Skulls and melted candles sat on a small table next to the bookcase. Roots and some sort of stinky vegetable hung from every inch of the ceiling, almost grazing Babette's head.

"Now, where did I leave that . . . Ah! Here it is." Babette took a heavy-looking book down from the shelf with both hands. "Magic is like cooking. Your outcome is only as good as your recipe, only as good as your ingredients and confidence in the kitchen, and only as good as your tools."

She walked out of the room, Lucely and Syd trailing her.

Babette set the book down gently on the table out in the library and opened it.

"This is the Spectral Master 4000. It's made of haunt-proof leather and can catch up to one hundred ghosts before needing to be purged," Babette said.

"I never knew Babette was a Ghostbuster." Lucely shook her head in awe.

"Humph. I am *not* a Ghostbuster, or a scientist. I'm a witch. It might have a techy name, but the Spectral Master 4000 is very much tied to magic. I just thought I might be able to sell them on eBay someday, and I needed something catchy to call them."

The book had three tiny buttons on it—catch, contain, and release—along with one light beneath each word. It had what looked like a heavy latch on two ends and a handle on the spine.

"How does it work?" asked Lucely.

"You have to get the ghost to float over it while the catch mechanism is engaged." Babette pointed to the button. "That sounds simple, but the button only stays engaged for thirty seconds. Then the trap reboots itself, and it won't work for another two minutes."

"Why did you make this so complicated?" Syd let her head fall to the table.

Babette bristled. "Containing magic is hard enough, let alone figuring out how to catch a ghost in the first place. Besides this is better than those raggedy mason jars you were using. *This* actually works. We just have to be smart about how we set the trap."

"I'm sorry, did you say *we*?" Syd didn't bother to lift her forehead from the table.

"Yes, *we*. I'm not about to let you girls go looking for the rest of those spells on your own. It's dangerous," Babette said. "You need a guide—someone who knows what they're doing. Besides, I'm old and bored. Now let me see what else you have in that bag of yours."

Syd carefully laid out all her stuff, and Lucely took her amulet from her pocket and put it on the table next to the other mason jar, the Florida water, the salt, and the candles.

Babette picked the amulets up one by one and weighed them in her hands. Then she held them up to her ear and shook each one before putting it down. She nodded in approval before moving on to the other items.

"This is all fine, except for the mason jars," she said.

Syd scowled. "So much jar hate."

"If there's only one Spectral Master 4000, how are Syd and I supposed to help?" asked Lucely.

"You will each have your own, but it won't look like this." Babette sat with a flourish, her long dress fluttering behind her as she settled into her claw-foot chair. "The best magic always has a personal element to it. This was my favorite book growing up, and its power lies not only in the spell I cast over it but also in the book's significance to me. I can do the same for the two of you with objects of sentimentality."

Lucely smiled. She already knew what her item would be, but she would have to go home to retrieve it.

Syd had a confused look on her face. "Literally the only thing I care about that much is Luce, and maybe Chunk. But neither of them are *things*."

Babette picked Chunk up with a groan and held her in front of Syd's face.

"The amulet you put on her collar works."

"Won't she get hurt?" Syd asked.

Babette threw her head back and laughed. "You'll sooner get hurt than Chunk."

Lucely and Syd looked at each other.

"Is Chunk . . . magic?" Lucely asked. "Because it almost seems like she told you where we were when she ran away." Lucely felt silly even suggesting it, but it *was* suspicious. The cat had disappeared at the cemetery, and then Babette had come to save them as if she'd been warned.

"I guess you could put it that way. Let's just say all my cats have something special about them. So, don't you worry about Chunk. I'd feel much safer with her near you anyway."

"Cool. You're my sidekick, Chunk. You hear that?" Syd scratched the cat's chin, and she immediately rolled over to show her ample belly, purring as she did.

"We should get her a cool T-shirt or something to solidify her new ghost-hunting status," Lucely said.

"Oh my gosh, maybe I can get my mom to make a little leather jacket to make her look like she's in some sort of cat biker gang!"

"Focus." Babette clapped her hands, pulling a book from the wall to reveal another secret compartment on the opposite side of the room. She shot a warning glance toward the girls. "This is not for anyone else to know. Understood?"

Lucely nodded, and Babette glided to the other side of the room. She reached inside the small, safe-like compartment that had opened, and pulled out a rolled-up parchment, putting two stones on either end of the scroll to hold it in place.

"This is a map of St. Augustine from 1832, marking every cemetery in town," Babette said. "The older the cemetery, the more likely it is to contain a considerable amount of magic and the more likely we are to find the missing pages. The plan is this: Cover every cemetery between now and the full moon on Halloween. Once that night comes, the spirits in town will likely gain enough strength that we won't be able to stop them, no matter how many ghost catchers I make."

"What happens once we catch the ghosts? Do they just stay in the catchers forever?" Lucely asked.

"No, we send them back to the underworld. I have a spell for that, don't you worry. Or well, I will."

"You don't have the spell yet?" Lucely asked.

"There are spells we could use, but I can put the spell together myself. Any spell that comes from inside me will be more powerful. I'll need an item of sentimental value from you, Luce, something I can turn into a real ghost catcher. Not all the ghosts around town are necessarily *evil*—some have just been rerouted, lost. It's the spirit monsters in the cemeteries I'm worried about." Babette rubbed her chin as if she were deep in thought. She clapped her hands together, her eyes lighting up as she did. "Do you know how you attract a ghost?"

Lucely and Syd shook their heads.

"Light." Babette flourished her hand and a small blue wisp of light appeared above her fingertips. As she spoke, she moved her fingers and the light danced around her elegant hands. "Magical light will attract a spirit that has lost its way."

Lucely opened her eyes wide. "That is the coolest thing I have ever seen."

"My family is the weirdest. I love it." Syd closed her eyes and sighed dramatically.

"I'll work on amplifying the power of Chunk's collar amulet for you, Syd. And Lucely, we can get your item first thing in the morning. Do you know what you'll use?"

Lucely nodded.

"Okay, I'll have all the necessary equipment ready to go by tomorrow morning. You'll each carry a flashlight and a ghost catcher and be wearing an amulet." Babette reached out and held Lucely's and Syd's hands. "We have to take every precaution so that you girls won't get hurt. Your parents will kill me if you are. But we need to help Lucely—and save the town."

"I can't believe we're gonna be a real-life ghost-catching gang," Lucely said.

"*Gang* is a good word for it." Babette said. "I haven't been in one of those since I was a kid."

Syd scrunched her nose. "I think *squad* sounds better."

"Fine, Ghost Squad it is, then." Babette smiled.

"Will you finally teach me how to be a witch now, Gran? I've been asking for years."

"And I've been telling you for years, being a witch isn't something just anyone can learn. If you show signs of magic one day, then I will."

"Ugh." Syd slumped her shoulders.

"What will we do once we get to the cemeteries?" asked Lucely.

"We will set up special crystal chimes that detect any ghostly activity and create as big of a perimeter of safety as we can while we search. The crystals will let us know if anything is coming our way so that we can prepare for a showdown. We'll check each mausoleum and also a few hidden spots I know of in each area."

"And if a baddie comes at us?" Syd quirked an eyebrow.

"You open your traps, press the button, and run like a pack of hornets is on your tail," Babette said, laughing.

"We can't just leave you to face them alone," said Lucely.

"You sure can, and you will, or the deal is off." Babette was firmer this time.

"We need more than just 'run' as a defense. What if your spells don't work or you get overwhelmed by ghosts? Then what?" Syd asked.

Babette sighed, clearly exasperated. "I will think about it, but you do make a valid point, granddaughter of mine.

"I have an idea. Something I'm not sure you'd feel comfortable with." Babette turned to Lucely. "Would you be able to bring a few of your fireflies? Your gift of sight might be enhanced with them around."

"Sight?" Lucely arched an eyebrow.

"The ability to see the other side, to see the spirits. Right now, there is a surge in supernatural power because of the spell, but normally people wouldn't be able to see beyond the veil. You can. It's a gift."

"My father . . . he said he could see them too when he was younger," Lucely said.

"Gifts and curses are usually passed on." Babette smiled.

"Lucely is pretty weird. It's why we're best friends," said Syd, puffing up her chest proudly.

"Yes, well, birds of a feather." Babette waved her hands around. "As I was saying, Lucely, would you be willing to bring a few of them with you?"

Lucely bit her lip. "So long as they'll be okay . . . But do you really think they'll be able to help at all?"

Babette opened her eyes wide. "They'll be able to fight, spirit versus spirit, to protect us and to push the ghosts back, returning them to their resting places."

"Wow," Syd and Lucely said together.

"And here I thought they were only good for being Lucely's sole friends besides me," Syd joked.

Lucely pushed her playfully. "Shut up, Syd. I just never thought of the fireflies as ghosts in the same way the scary ghosts from the cemeteries are. I mean, they're not scary, not usually anyway. Not before the past few weeks. Does it matter which fireflies I bring?"

"If there are any you think might be especially good in sticky situations, bring them," Babette said.

Lucely nodded, thinking of who would be best. Celestino came to mind, her uncle who made booby traps. Tía Milagros could put the fear of God into anyone's heart. And of course she'd bring Frankie, who had already saved them once. She tallied all the ghosts who might be helpful to her. By the time she wrote down all the names, she had fifteen on a list.

"You think this will be enough?" Lucely asked Babette, holding up the list.

"I think this is perfect." Babette smiled. "And, Lucely . . . there's something I need to tell you, both of you." Now Babette sounded deadly serious. "The spell you found from my book, it wasn't actually from my book. I mean, it was, but someone had altered it. They corrupted the spell—turned it into a deadly curse."

"Who would do something like that?" Syd asked.

Lucely looked at Syd, clearing her throat. "We saw the initials *E. B.* written next to the spell—do you know who they could've belonged to?"

Babette was quiet for a long time, a faraway look in her eyes. "Hmm . . . I do know of someone, but she died long ago. Her name was Eliza Braggs, a member of the Daughters of the American Revolution with a staunch hatred for anything that she deemed 'unnatural.' She publically accused Las Brujas Moradas of hexing her son—among other unexplained events—none of which was ever proven. Then she gathered a mob of townspeople and drove the coven out of St. Augustine for good."

Her attention snapped back to Lucely and Syd. "What Eliza did was cruel, but she's long gone now."

An air of silence fell over the room, and Lucely realized that they hadn't told Babette about Mayor Anderson and what they'd overheard at city hall.

"Is it possible that she could be behind all this?" Lucely asked. "Like, trying to exact revenge or something?"

"What do you mean?" Babette asked.

"Umm . . . so we sort of spied on Mayor Anderson a little during our school trip." Lucely braced herself for yelling, but instead Babette just nodded as a signal to go on. "We saw him the first night in the cemetery when we recited the spell—at least we're pretty sure it was him. He went into the mausoleum after we'd run out."

"So, we decided to eavesdrop on his office at city hall," Syd added. "And we overheard a bunch of voices plotting some sort of attack at the Halloween Festival this weekend." Syd pulled the recorder out of her backpack and replayed the mayor's conversation.

"And maybe it was fear making me hallucinate, but I'm pretty sure the dragon-mist-monster looked just like him before he transformed into Drago," said Syd.

"Drago?" Babette hitched an eyebrow.

"Just a nickname I came up with for the dragon monster. You gotta admit, the thing was pretty cute."

Babette let out an exasperated breath. "Try not to become attached to the monsters attempting to kill us, Syd. But that *is* troubling. We can't be too careful. Stay away from Mayor Anderson. Even if he doesn't seem like a bad guy, it's possible he may be wrapped up in something nefarious, whether this has anything to do with Eliza Braggs or not. No more spying; it's too dangerous."

The look in Babette's eyes left no room for negotiation. "If this *is* Eliza, there must be a reason she led the two of you— someone with the gift of sight and someone with possible, just *possible*, ties to witchcraft—to recite the spell." Babette looked at Syd, who was beaming. "Whoever's behind this seems to have it all planned out. So be extra careful—and trust no one."

CHAPTER EIGHTEEN

EARLY THE NEXT MORNING, Babette drove Lucely to her house to pick up Mamá's mason jar from her bedside. Lucely knew of nothing else as valuable to her in the world.

Before they left, Babette said a protection spell over the willow tree.

"The magic contained in this tree is ancient," Babette said. "Much more powerful than anything I'm capable of conjuring. But I hope this helps a little."

A few hours later, Babette called them into her living room and plopped a box on the floor in front of them. "I made something for you girls."

Lucely looked in the box and gasped.

"Go on, take one," Babette said.

She picked up one of the black denim jackets and shrugged it on. The back had a ghost patch sewn on and the words *Ghost Squad* stitched above it in purple lettering.

"This is so cool!" Lucely admired herself in a full-length mirror in Babette's living room.

Syd held up her own jacket. "This is the most beautiful thing I've ever seen."

There was even a cat-size one for Chunk.

Babette was the last to put her jacket on, and with her dark jeans, black T-shirt, and long gray dreadlocks, Lucely was pretty sure she was the coolest person she'd seen in her entire life.

"There's more," said Babette, handing Lucely her mason jar and Syd, Chunk. The mason jar had a slight, glittery sheen to it, and it smelled like dried roses. The amulet shone brightly from Chunk's neck, and she purred as Syd inspected it.

"Come on, we need a picture," Babette said, setting up her camera.

They posed with their respective ghost catchers, Chunk sitting smack in the middle of them on the floor. Lucely made her best tough face, and when they reviewed the picture, it seemed they all had. They looked like some sort of ragtag biker gang.

A warm feeling spread through Lucely, something like belonging. And love. She felt like she was becoming part of an even bigger family, like Babette might be her own grandmother. But no sooner had the thought entered her brain than Lucely began feeling guilty. After all, her own grandmother was sick or cursed. She wouldn't let herself forget that.

The sun had long since set by the time Syd, Babette, and Lucely struck out to their first destination in Babette's old station wagon, with wooden paneling on the side and a license plate that read ETMYDUST.

Syd climbed into the back of the car as Chunk jumped onto the seat next to Babette.

"I guess Chunk called shotgun," Lucely said, sliding in next to Syd.

"That cat's more her granddaughter than I am." Syd gave Lucely a sideways glance, clicking her seat belt into place.

"I can hear everything and see everything," Babette said.

Lucely opened her eyes and mouth wide in mock fear, and Syd laughed so loud Chunk hissed.

Babette turned the radio on, and a pop song about heartbreak blared through the speakers. They all, including a mewing Chunk, sang at the top of their lungs, pumping themselves up for the night to come. But as they got closer to the cemetery, Babette turned the radio down and a somber mood fell over them.

Respect the spirits, Lucely remembered, and closed her eyes, her hands wrapped around her ghost catcher. She said a silent prayer to whoever or whatever was watching over them, and she hoped they could protect her, Syd, Babette, and Chunk from whatever was coming their way tonight.

"I put packets of salt in my dad's fanny pack and sprinkled some in his shoes," Lucely told Syd. "I hope it's enough to keep any ghost monsters from hurting him."

"Babette also gave him a few charms and stuff for the customers. They'll think it's all for show, but if they're wearing amulets, then it's a lot less likely for anything weird to happen." Syd put her hand on Lucely's and squeezed. "Not much else we can do that we're not already trying to do, Luce."

Things seemed pretty bleak, but the gesture filled Lucely with hope. The mere fact that she wasn't alone in trying to figure this all out was enough to comfort her, for now.

A heavy fog had settled on the ground by the time they approached the entrance of St. Augustine Memorial Cemetery, and it looked as if they were standing on a bed of clouds.

Lucely was grateful for her jacket now and that Babette had convinced her to wear jeans instead of shorts.

The iron gate had a heavy-looking chain wrapped around two bars at its center.

"Close your eyes, you two," Babette instructed.

Lucely closed her eyes most of the way but looked over to Syd, who also had one eye slightly open to watch whatever it was Babette was about to do.

Babette placed her hands on the padlocked gate, creating a soft purple glow. Seconds later, the lock simply popped open and the chain slithered away into a nearby bush as if it were a snake. Babette looked back at the girls with a hitched eyebrow.

"You can open your eyes all the way now, you sneaks."

Lucely laughed nervously, and Syd's mouth was open wide enough to fit a football in it.

"Gram, I am insulted that you never told me you could do that."

"If I sat there telling you all the things I know and you don't, we'd never get up. Now come on."

Lucely and Syd trailed Babette as she led them into the graveyard, Syd whispering questions about magic the entire way as Babette waved her off.

They stopped beside a concrete bench, and Babette turned to them with her Spectral Master 4000 in hand.

"Everyone got their ghost catcher?"

Lucely held up her jar. Syd held up a wriggling Chunk with some difficulty.

"All right, let's go find that spell," Babette said.

Beams from their flashlights intersected as they walked as quietly as they could through the cemetery, trying their best to avoid all the crunchy dead leaves. Chunk had settled into the baby carrier on Syd's chest, her whiskers tickling at Syd's nostrils and threatening to bring on a sneeze attack.

"This cat is so dang heavy," Syd complained, swatting at her whiskers.

They reached the first mausoleum, and again Babette used her purple light magic to unlock the doors. Babette looked back at Lucely and Syd. "Any chance I can convince you to stay outside while I search?"

"Not even a little," Syd said.

Lucely shrugged. "Babette, I know you're way more capable than we are, but we did do this on our own before. Plus, it's only fair we help out since it is sort of all our fault."

Babette breathed out through her nose. "*Sort of*? Ha. Follow me," she whispered as she stepped into the dark crypt.

In the middle of the round room sat a wooden casket with gold clasps and hinges. Babette ran her finger along the top of it before inspecting it with her flashlight. No dust, Lucely saw. The door was definitely sealed. Otherwise, that mountain of dust would not have erupted when Babette opened it.

"So why is this casket clean?" Lucely shook despite herself, a chill penetrating to her bones.

"Why indeed," Babette considered.

"Let's open it." Syd gestured toward the casket.

Babette shook her head. "I don't think we should; something feels off about this place."

"Aren't we *looking* for something off?" Syd asked.

"Something magical, yes, but not something evil. I think I should do a cleansing ritual in here before . . ."

"*RAAAAAAAAAAA!*"

Lucely grabbed Syd's arm, and they both screamed. Babette whipped her flashlight around the crypt.

"Who's there?" she demanded.

"*RAAAAAAAAAAA!*" the thing said again.

Syd made for the door, but Lucely stopped her. "Don't go alone, remember?"

"So come with me, and let's get the heck outta here!"

"Wait, come and stand behind me," Babette said. "It's not safe. Lucely is right."

Lucely felt her way over to Babette, careful not to touch the casket. The light from her flashlight seemed suddenly dim, not bright enough to break the heavy darkness around them. Something was definitely wrong. Very wrong.

"There must be something hiding here," whispered Babette. "We shouldn't anger the spirits, but we should recognize when a sign is sent our way. Salt shakers at the ready."

Lucely grabbed her container of salt from her pocket.

"Go stand in the far corner to our right and make a circle of salt around the both of you," Babette said. "Don't step outside it, no matter what happens."

"But, Gram—" Syd started, and stopped once she saw the look Babette leveled at her.

"What about our ghost catchers?" Lucely asked.

"Keep them with you in case . . . in case the salt is not enough."

Lucely nodded, trying to be braver than she felt. The truth was that she'd give anything to be under her covers right now with a book about a boy wizard, instead of living an adventure where he'd be a lot more useful than she was. But she did as Babette instructed. Standing in the middle of a salt circle with Syd and Chunk, Lucely wielded her ghost catcher, ready to capture anything that came their way.

Something cold swept through the room and their flashlights blinked out, plunging them into a thick blackness. Syd frantically clicked the switch on her flashlight, but instead of the light coming back on, candles lining the perimeter of the mausoleum flickered on.

Lucely rubbed her eyes. "Do you also see candles everywhere?"

"Yep." Syd nodded. "I'm not scared *at all*."

Lucely's nerves were getting the best of her. She'd grown up around spirits, but she had never in all her life experienced anything like *this*.

Babette turned to them, now fully illuminated by candlelight, and held one finger up to her lips.

"*Babette . . .*" A raspy voice filled the room. "*Why have you come here to disturb my sleep?*"

Lucely froze. She felt Syd go deathly still beside her, and she searched for her hand wildly, not daring to look anywhere but straight ahead.

"I didn't mean to disturb you," Babette's voice rang out clearly, calmly. "We were only searching for something . . . missing pages from a book."

"*A book you say?*" The voice sounded amused. "*Why, I believe you must be lost. This isn't the library.*"

"It's a special kind of book, one that contains a spell. A spell to return the dead to their home."

Syd squeezed Lucely's hand. Lucely's eyes watered with fear.

"*Why would I help you send us back there when we're having such a grand old time here?*" The voice laughed maniacally.

A burst of cold hit Lucely from the back, knocking her to the ground.

The candles' flames grew so high, they almost touched the ceiling.

Lucely tried to get up, but something kept her legs pressed to the ground.

"Babette!" she cried out just as something made of smoke dove toward her, stopping right in front of her face.

The figure was inhuman except for two red, glowing eyes staring back at Lucely and a mouth like an open wound. It smelled like death.

She couldn't move her arms or legs; she couldn't even cry out for help. Beside her, Syd looked as if she was in shock. She watched as the figure jolted to the side, a flash of purple light pinning it to the far wall.

Lucely struggled to her feet and tried to get Syd up as well, but her friend seemed lost in another world.

"Syd, come on, get up," Lucely pleaded as she tried again to pull Syd up from her place on the ground. But it was no use. Instead, Lucely grabbed the salt container from her pocket and redrew the circle to encompass Syd.

"Back in the circle, Lucely!" Babette instructed as she fought off the monster.

Lucely had always done as she was told, had always listened to her father, had always tried to be good. Now she had to do the opposite of what Babette was asking. She knew she did, or it might be the end—for all of them.

Lucely opened her ghost catcher instead and charged into the swirling mass. It felt much like it had when Mamá had gone through her body, except worse—so much worse. This spirit was filled with anger and hate. Years and years of it, pent up, was now surging through her. She just hoped she'd pressed the capture button in time.

Noise like a vacuum choking on a hair tie erupted all around her.

Lucely opened her eyes, and the evil spirit was gone.

Her legs gave out from under her, and she dropped painfully to her knees.

"Are you okay?" Babette asked when she reached Lucely's side.

Lucely was dazed but nodded slowly.

"Don't you ever do something that foolish again, Lucely Luna!" Babette wrapped her in a tight embrace. "Though, I have to say . . . that was quite impressive. But I'm afraid there are still more corrupted spirits lurking here. I can feel their presence. Come on then, we haven't got much time to keep searching."

With a splash of something from Babette's bag on her face, Syd woke up from her trance.

"Figures I'd miss the good stuff," she said.

"Help me get this open." Babette signaled to the casket.

The large casket opened with a low groan, and inside they found the remains of a skeleton in musty clothing, a brittle piece of rolled parchment still in its grasp.

CHAPTER NINETEEN

"THAT WAS A DISASTER," proclaimed Lucely. "We could've been murdered."

Babette swept into the loft carrying a tray of hot cocoa and cookies. She placed it in the center of the table, where Lucely and Syd were waiting for her.

All of Babette's cats lay on the top bunk of one of the beds, their little heads peering over the edge at them, lined neatly in a row.

"I don't think ghosts can murder you. I think, at best, they possess you and drag you into the underworld," said Babette.

"Oh, right, okay. That's *so* much better, Gram." Syd took a bite of a cookie and shook her head. "What's the plan, then? We can't exactly run around town as ghost bait all night while you search every casket."

"We have a spirit map now. A map that will hopefully lead us to the spell if we follow its instructions."

"What instructions?" asked Lucely.

Babette pulled the rolled-up paper from a pocket in her gown and unfurled it on the table in front of them. They sat in a circle, looking down at the map.

"Here." Babette pointed to the small red dot that marked Tolomato Cemetery. "I think this is where we should go next."

When they left St. Augustine Memorial Cemetery, the dot marking its location on the map faded to a light brown. The map didn't have much detail to it, but Lucely knew the layout of St. Augustine like she knew Syd's favorite food was macaroni and cheese. "Do you think the spirit map is trying to point us to the next destination?"

"Certainly seems plausible," Babette said. "It looks like those are the only two locations that have been marked. Which means that either more will appear as we progress or the pages must be somewhere in Tolomato Cemetery."

Just as Babette was starting to roll up the map, Lucely saw a flash of red at its edge, near the old lighthouse, but when she looked again it was gone. Chunk yawned and rolled onto her back. "You're right, Chunk. I'm probably just tired."

"Gram, listen." Syd jumped up and grabbed a handful of Oreos from the cookie jar. "What if you taught us to fight?

Nothing too advanced—and not witchy stuff—but enough to kick some major ghost butt!"

Syd held up her hands in a show of surrender at the look Babette gave her. "You said Lucely's firefly spirits could fight back. We just want to help out! Also, most of the ghosts in town are just people who used to live here. You must know some of them, Gram."

"Syd Faires, you better not be calling me old . . ." Babette arched an eyebrow threateningly.

"It's a good thing. Age is wisdom, blah, blah, blah. This could work in our favor!"

Lucely bit her lip. "If it worked, I bet we'd have a much better shot at winning this thing. We're not quite ghost-hunting amateurs anymore, but if we are attacked the way that one ghost came at us at the cemetery, we'll probably die."

"We would definitely die. We would one hundred percent die. Dead, toast. Then it'd be up to you to send us into the underworld, Gram, and I am going to be the most annoying ghost of all time! And—"

"Enough, I get it. You don't have to remind me how annoying you can be when I have you right here." Babette took a sharp breath. "I can try to send out a spirit signal. It might not work, but we can try."

Syd threw her arms around Babette's neck and hugged her. Lucely's face went hot. She felt awkward watching their family moment. Just as she started to turn away, Babette pulled her into a group hug. Chunk mewed, jumping down from the bunk bed, and tried to wiggle her way in too.

"We're gonna have to quickly level you two up if we plan on whooping Eliza's ghost army tomorrow night." Babette stood up. "Meet me out back in five."

Babette's backyard was enclosed by a dense perimeter of trees and hedges, concealing it from what she liked to call Nosy Nellies. Strings of light spanned the width of the lawn, making the property look like Lucely imagined a fairy glen would. The pleasant aroma of lavender and rosemary carried over from the herb garden. Syd launched herself onto the cushioned swing that hung from an ancient-looking oak, almost causing the entire thing to collapse.

Babette appeared moments later, two skinny flashlights in hand.

"We're going to protect ourselves against evil spirits with flashlights?" Syd asked.

"Hush, child. They're not flashlights," Babette said. "I haven't used these in many years, but they're powerful weapons. *Magic* weapons."

"*Omg omg omg omg,*" Syd whispered under her breath. Lucely wiped her sweaty hands on her pants.

Babette handed one to Lucely and the other to Syd.

"Don't touch any of the buttons," she said. "Just look it over while I explain."

The flashlights were much heavier than they looked. They had a chrome finish and deep grooves that gave them a vintage look, almost like lightsabers.

"I call these beauties my Razzle-Dazzlers. They are capable of stunning any supernatural being within a ten-foot radius. You don't wanna get caught in the beam though or um . . ." Babette rubbed her neck. "Let's just say it wouldn't be pretty."

Lucely's eyes widened. "Noted."

"All right now, careful not to hit the trees," Babette said. "There might be birds in there."

"On three?" Lucely asked, and Syd nodded.

"One . . . two . . . three!"

When they pressed the button, a brilliant rainbow-colored light emitted from the Razzle-Dazzlers, casting a wash of pink, blue, and purple over the entire backyard.

"Okay, off, off. Don't waste the juice," Babette said. "We don't have time for a training montage, but, in my experience, the best way to learn fast is in the real world. Now let's go hunt some ghosts."

Something in the air changed the moment they entered Tolomato Cemetery. It was close enough to freezing that even though Lucely had buttoned her Ghost Squad jacket all the way up, the hairs in her nose felt like tiny icicles. Even Macarena's firefly appeared to be shivering inside her mason jar.

"It's colder than the mashed potatoes in the cafeteria out here," Syd said, her teeth chattering.

Chunk mewed angrily.

Babette positioned Lucely and Syd around a ring of flickering candles and instructed them to hold hands. "For this spell to work, you will have to close your eyes. I want you to pour every ounce of good energy, thoughts, and feelings you can muster into the circle."

Lucely closed her eyes and thought of her father. She thought of Mamá and of Syd, of summers spent playing at the beach and of nights lying out beneath the willow tree, watching her firefly spirits for hours. She thought of curling up with her favorite book and a cup of the Dominican hot cocoa her abuela used to make. Waves of energy radiated from within her as she imagined pushing it all into the space within their held hands.

"Open your eyes," Babette said.

Radiant bands of golden light danced before them, intertwined like living vines.

"Whoa." Lucely and Syd were transfixed.

With a flourish of her hand, Babette released the light,

allowing it to spread out across the cemetery. Babette turned toward them. "There's a dark energy here, something dangerous. I believe the map has led us here for a reason, either to find the spell we need or to draw us into a lethal trap."

"Well, now I'm feeling *much* better about this whole 'real-world experience' thing." Lucely turned to Syd, who was nuzzling Chunk with her nose.

"She *does* have a way with words," Syd said. "It's the Faires flare."

Lucely sighed. "Can we bring back the happy lights?"

"Let's get going before the protection spell breaks," Babette said as the girls followed behind her. "I stored a magical item here years ago for safekeeping, and it might come in handy."

"Who stores their stuff in a cemetery?" Syd whispered to Lucely.

"Your grandmother, apparently." Lucely patted her jacket pocket, making sure her Razzle-Dazzler was still there. "Don't tell Babette, but I'm kinda hoping a ghost pops up so we can use these things."

"You're telling me," grumbled Syd.

Babette halted when they came to an oddly shaped hill, too tall and narrow to be natural. She let her hand graze along the moss-covered surface, circling the mound until an opening appeared before them. "In here."

Lucely and Syd followed silently.

The space lit up with a dim, warm light from the camping lantern Babette had brought with her, and Lucely's eyes slowly adjusted to her new surroundings. It was a small, round room with no outlet except the entrance they'd come through.

Lucely ran her hand along the dirt wall, marveling at how the dome didn't collapse under the weight of the earth, when her fingers brushed against something solid. She brushed some of the dirt aside to reveal *bones*.

"Oh my gosh. Is this . . . a *catacomb*?" Lucely sucked in a breath as she shook her hand to get the bone germs off her. Chunk mewed.

"Oh yeah, you might not want to touch the walls. I forgot to tell you that," Babette said absentmindedly as she walked around the room, eyes closed.

"Any luck with, uh, whatever it is that you're looking f—"

Babette held one hand up, cutting her off. With her eyes still closed, she held out her other hand, palm facing down, and tilted her head slightly as if she were concentrating really hard.

Nothing happened at first, but then the ground began to shudder. Lucely jumped behind Babette, her Razzle-Dazzler at the ready.

Dirt exploded from the floor, getting in Lucely's eyes and mouth, and she was pretty sure some made its way into her pants too. By the time she was able to open her eyes, Babette was holding a shiny object before them: a small black arrow.

"That doesn't really look like a magical item," Syd said. "What is it?"

"This is a Finder-Keeper. It helps you find something—anything you want—by pointing you in the direction of it." Babette smiled. "If we think of the missing pages with this in hand, we can find them! Come, we have to get to higher ground for it to work properly."

As they made their way out of the catacomb, heavy footsteps bounded up behind them.

Lucely and Syd turned—ready to attack—and came face-to-face with Chunk. Literally.

Somehow, Chunk had grown so she was the same size as Lucely and Syd. Then, in a deep voice as smooth as silk, Chunk spoke: "Run."

Babette grabbed Lucely and Syd by the arms and pulled them along before they were able to react. The sound of a shrieking train barreled toward them from across the graveyard, hurricane-force winds on its heels.

"What happened to Chunk?" Lucely shrieked. "Why are we running?"

"I think that if Chunk grew five times her normal size and spoke like Lionel Richie, we should probably just trust her and go," Syd screamed back.

Lucely tried to keep up with Babette, who was a

surprisingly fast runner, but her feet kept sinking into muddy patches of soil. A sharp pain pierced Lucely's chest.

The air froze around them as they approached a giant oak tree. Babette stopped, leaning against it to steady herself.

"Get your weapons out." Babette took the lead, standing in front of Lucely and Syd with her hands up.

Lucely held her Razzle-Dazzler up and willed her knees not to buckle beneath her. The night was suddenly deadly still, quiet. Babette's hands trembled slightly, Lucely observed. That couldn't be a good sign.

"Get behind me, girls," Babette instructed, but neither of them stepped back.

"We won't let you face it alone," Lucely said. "All for one . . ."

"And one for all," Syd continued, just as a giant mist monster materialized before them.

"Okay," Babette swallowed. "On my signal."

The creature charged, the air around it crackling with static energy. Every step it took shook the ground.

Before it could overtake them, Babette screamed, "GIVE 'EM THE OLD RAZZLE-DAZZLE!"

Lucely and Syd engaged their Razzle-Dazzlers at the same time, sending two pulses of rainbow light arcing out and converging with the purple beam of energy Babette had conjured.

The mist monster vanished in a shriek of pain.

"Where'd it go?" Lucely asked, spinning in circles searching for any signs of attack.

"Did we defeat i—"

Before Syd could celebrate, the monster reappeared, attacking them so fast that none of them had time to react.

Babette was no longer standing at the ready next to Lucely and Syd. Now she was suspended in the center of the creature's belly—at least where its belly would be if it weren't a hideous, see-through beast.

"NO!" Syd screamed, pointing her Razzle-Dazzler at the mist monster that had enveloped her grandmother.

"No, Syd, don't shoot. You don't know what that thing will do to Babette." Lucely's mind raced. "I know you're scared. I am too. But if we're gonna save Babette, we have to be smart about this. You're not alone; I'm here."

Syd tore her eyes from Babette, her face creased with despair. Lucely's hand flew to the fireflies at her side. She put her Razzle-Dazzler in her back pocket and turned back toward Syd.

"I'm going to use the fireflies to lure the mist monster away from Babette. Once it lets her go—only once it lets her go—you shoot it with all the power that Razzle-Dazzler's got left. Okay?" Lucely put one hand on Syd's shoulder. "You can do this, Syd."

Syd nodded, but Lucely could tell she was still terrified.

Lucely hugged her before running out into the open to face the mist monster.

"I need some help, guys," she whispered to the tiny lights in her mason jar. They flickered in response, and a surge of warm energy seemed to run from them to Lucely.

"Hey, ugly! Over here!" Lucely opened her mason jar, and the fireflies surrounded her, creating a whirlpool of light.

The monster turned toward her and smiled.

This thing had Babette. This thing might kill Babette. This thing was coming right at her.

Lucely planted her feet firmly, remembering the way Mamá's feet in the vision seemed to be rooted to the willow tree, how she grew large and was made of fury and light and love. She let that feeling fill her now, fire burning inside her heart.

The monster barreled toward her, and behind it, she could see Babette lying on the ground where it had left her.

Lucely forced herself not to scream, closing her eyes and praying for her fireflies' protection.

A burst of rainbow light shot through the air and straight into the monster's chest, banishing it into the night.

Syd collapsed to her knees next to Babette.

"Is she okay?" Lucely yelled as she ran over to them.

"She's breathing," Syd said in a small voice. "But she needs a doctor. Or a witch doctor, or something! How are we gonna get her out of here? It's not like either of us can drive—or even carry her for that matter."

"I have an idea," Lucely said, before calling Macarena out. If the attack at the barrack was any indication, she could always be depended on to help. Lucky for them, she also knew how to drive, though that had been decades ago when she was alive.

"Claro que si, yes, I will help," she said once Lucely had explained their predicament. Macarena used her firefly magic to carry Babette, floating through the misty night, to the car.

"I really hope there's no one watching," Lucely said. "They'd probably be scarred for life watching an old lady floating through a cemetery."

"If they survived the mist monster, they can survive seeing this," Syd laughed.

"Go back to the hillside, you dolts."

An icy chill ran down Lucely's back. "Who's there?"

"The missing pages—the monster was guarding the missing pages," Babette continued.

"Gram!" Syd was standing over Babette in a flash, stroking her hair.

"Lucely, run. Before the other ghosts get wind of the mist monster being gone. Here." She placed the Finder-Keeper in Lucely's hand. "It was pointing back toward the catacomb before that thing showed up. It's gotta be in there somewhere. I'll be fine. Now go, child! It's up to you."

Lucely took a deep breath, bracing herself before entering the catacombs again. Inside, it was pitch-black save for the dim glow of her flashlight reflecting off the bones lining the walls.

She held the Finder-Keeper out in the palm of her hand as she had seen Babette do and closed her eyes. Lucely concentrated on the missing spell, Las Brujas Moradas, the torn-out pages. She bit her lip, one eye still shut, hoping something would happen.

The arrow began to shudder, coming alive and hovering just above Lucely's hand before spinning wildly.

"Okay, thingamajig, you're supposed to point me in the direction of the missing pages, and this is definitely not helping."

The arrow came to a sudden stop, as if it had heard her, and was pointing to a spot directly above her. The rounded ceiling of the catacomb was completely covered in skulls.

"This is just the worst," Lucely muttered.

She scanned the constellation of bones looking for anything out of place, but the skulls all looked nearly identical. Frustrated, Lucely collapsed in a huff on the ground. Then she noticed that the eyes of one of the skulls seemed to twinkle. She stood on her tippy-toes to get as close as she could to the glittering skull and saw two obsidian gemstones inset where there should only be hollow sockets.

"Aha!" Lucely said to herself, grabbing a rock and taking aim to try to knock it loose. Her first attempt landed just two skulls over. She tried again, but the second rock hit even farther away than the first. Shaking her head, Lucely gripped another rock in her hand and took a deep breath, steadying herself.

Come on, Lucely. You got this. Just pretend you're throwing a dodgeball right at Tilly Maxwell.

She closed her eyes and pictured a bull's-eye in the space between the skull's eyes. When she released the third stone, it hit the target dead-on and the skull broke free from the ceiling.

Lucely picked up the skull from the ground and inspected the smooth surface, searching for any other clues that made this skull special. Aside from the gemstones, it looked normal. Well, as normal as Lucely had imagined a real skull would look this up close and personal. The gemstones reminded Lucely of *The Goonies*. She quickly tested one of them, thinking it might well be enough to help her dad get out of trouble with the bank, but the gems were fused to the skull and wouldn't budge.

Lucely could sense a shift in the air outside the catacomb the longer she stayed inside. She held the skull as close to her ear as she could without it touching her and shook it gently—there was a faint sound of something moving within.

Cold crept into the room now, and Lucely's breath came out in a white fog. The evil spirits were getting closer. She didn't want to break the skull, so she tried to pull whatever was inside, out from a small crack. Panic crept over her as she struggled, her heart racing until finally she got a small scroll of paper out.

Lucely didn't have time to attempt to decipher the barely legible script, so she stuffed it into her pocket and fled into the night.

CHAPTER TWENTY

BY THE TIME THE MORNING sun filtered into Babette's library, Lucely and Syd had been able to figure out only the beginnings of the spell. They had stayed up the rest of the night attempting to figure out a solution to their spell dilemma. They read through dozens of Babette's books, splicing bits from one spell and parts of another. But it was like trying to put together an impossible puzzle with instructions in another language.

The scroll of paper Lucely had found in the catacomb didn't make any sense.

"A light to guide you through the night,
Confront your fate before it's too late."

Syd repeated the words over and over, hoping it would magically click something into place, but nothing worked.

Babette joined them once she'd recovered from being attacked, but even she couldn't figure out the right spell.

"What are we going to do if we can't figure out the rest of the spell before the Halloween Festival tonight?" Lucely asked.

"I don't know. We face Eliza and hold her off for as long as we can." Babette sounded defeated. "Let's hear what you have so far, girls."

Lucely and Syd looked at each other and nodded.

"A sprinkle of sun,
A shimmer of light,
Turn back the darkness,
Turn back the fright . . ."

The spirits were silent as Babette closed her eyes and took in a deep breath, feeling the air around her like she was searching for something in the dark.

"That is . . . surprisingly powerful. Well done."

They both yawned, and Lucely felt the weight of the night before dragging her down. She hadn't realized how tired she was, the adrenaline of trying to figure out the spell must've been keeping her awake.

Babette must've noticed because she got up and ushered them out of the library and up to the loft. "Get some rest, girls. We're going to need all the energy we can muster tonight."

Sometime during the day, while Babette and the girls recovered from the mist monster battle, a hurricane-force storm had arrived at St. Augustine's front door.

By the time they left for the Halloween Festival, the sky was blanketed with dark gray clouds, obscuring the light of the full moon. Decorations were being ripped from the lampposts and trees by the violent winds as Babette drove toward city hall. Lucely could feel the evil spirits bearing down on them, as if they were breathing down her neck.

Whoever was in charge of decorations this year had gone completely overboard. Somehow, they had managed to make the entire facade of the building look like an actual haunted house—creepy lighting, sound effects, and all.

Syd had the brilliant idea for her and Lucely to dress up as ghost hunters so that they could blend in with the rest of the costumed partygoers—not as the Phantom Hunters, but as the Ghost Squad.

The parking lot was packed, so Babette got creative. She revved her engine before driving right off the edge of the asphalt, coming to an abrupt stop on top of a hedgerow of bushes.

"If you can't find a parking spot, make one." Babette hopped out of the car, and they approached the Halloween Festival together. Cobwebs and oversize spiders decorated the balconies of the main hall. There were witches on broomsticks hanging from the ceiling, ghosts and shadowed monsters projected onto the walls, and even a live jazz band all dressed as mummies—with Syd's mother on drums and her father playing the sax. Thousands of costumed townspeople filled the main level of the hall, making it nearly impossible to pick out any familiar faces. But Lucely finally spotted her dad from across the room, dressed in the same Tin Man costume he wore every year, handing out fliers for the tour.

A wave of relief washed over her. After the weekend they'd had, she had to fight back tears at the sight of him.

"You two look great!" Simon beamed, approaching the girls. "Where's Babette?"

Syd pointed at Babette, who was eyeing everyone suspiciously near the punch bowl.

"I'll have my eyes on you two the whole time. No sneaking off. No adventures," Simon warned.

"Got it," Lucely said, and they walked into the large, brick town hall building together. If only he knew it was too late for warnings about adventures. Way too late.

Simon had been pulled away, handing Luna Ghost Tour pamphlets out to a group dressed like *Star Wars* characters, when the room suddenly became ten degrees cooler.

Lucely shivered—Syd must've felt it too, because she pressed closer to Lucely and took hold of her hand.

The hall was plunged into pitch-black darkness, a few people screamed, and then a solitary spotlight illuminated the landing of the imperial staircase where Mayor Anderson now stood, a menacing grin distorting his face. He looked around the grand hall as he spoke. "Welcome, welcome! It is always such a pleasure to host this spectacular event each year. We've spared no expense to ensure that this Halloween will be one that each of you will never forget."

Mayor Anderson's gaze settled on Lucely and Syd, eyes flickering.

Dark clouds began to form overhead, completely obscuring the high ceiling. They pulsed, heat lightning flashing within like strobe lights as thunder softly began to thrum a steady bass line. Dancing resumed on the main level of the floor, the partygoers entranced by what they thought was all a part of the show.

Just then, something caught Lucely's attention. "I don't think those are clouds, Syd."

As their eyes adjusted to the darkness, Lucely and Syd could see that the clouds seemed to be made up of not just mist and shadow but the writhing, wailing bodies of the undead.

Mayor Anderson's skin began to fade into a murky, translucent color like he was made of swamp water, his eyes glowing a sickly green, as he raised his arms like the conductor of an orchestra readying for an overture.

With a flash of lightning, he brought his hands down swiftly, and the dark clouds broke, unleashing a monsoon of spirits on the unsuspecting guests.

All around them, residents screamed and tried helplessly to swipe at the ghosts as if they were a swarm of bees. A stampede of townspeople fled the building as quickly as they could.

"Where's Babette?!" Syd screamed over the commotion.

"I don't know, but we have to do something!" Lucely whipped out her Razzle-Dazzler and fired off a few arcs of light.

Spirits descended into the crowd, and an older man was picked up and thrown onto the dessert table, but he got up and ran out the door a moment later. One woman was dangling upside down, an invisible force holding one of her ankles and shaking her so candy and loose change fell from her pockets as she screamed. A group of kids from Lucely's school shrieked in terror as spirits picked them up and swooped out of the room with them before Lucely or Syd had time to save them. Lucely's ghost catcher began to beep: It was close to capacity.

The spirits were attacking residents faster than Lucely and Syd could zap them. Cold bursts of air zoomed past as they ducked and weaved out of the way. They needed Babette; they needed an army.

"Now what?" Syd screamed over the ghosts' wails.

A flash of silver caught Lucely's eye—the unmistakable sight of her father's Tin Man costume.

"Pop, over here!" Lucely shouted, but her cries were drowned out by the wails of the spirit monsters.

The fireflies buzzed at her side, and Lucely's heart lurched. She knew they wanted to help, to protect her, but she was afraid to lose them.

"You don't have to do it alone because we are with you, always." Mamá's words came back to Lucely, just as her father reached her side.

"Dad," Lucely said, "there is a small jar clipped to my jeans. It has some of our fireflies in it. Unclip it and open it. The fireflies will know what to do."

She didn't have to look at her dad to feel the confusion radiating from his direction and all the questions he had for her, but instead of asking, he got to work. The moment Simon opened the jar, the fireflies flew out and gathered in a whirlwind of light, making a noise like water being poured onto a hot pan.

Lucely kept one eye on them and one eye on the ghosts and her rattling Razzle-Dazzler. Her father was still holding the small jar, his face like a kid's, soft and bright, full of wonder. Somehow, Lucely knew that he could again see the faces of his lost family members flashing in the light.

At the same time as Lucely, he saw the one face they both missed more than anything: Mamá Teresa, his mother.

"Mamá," Lucely whispered, transfixed, her Razzle-Dazzler dropping to her side.

"Luce!" Simon and Syd screamed at once, and Lucely raised her Razzle-Dazzler up. But it was too late. A mob of ghosts surged toward her, their mouths open wide and ready to attack.

The ghosts pinned her down to the wooden floor, and she felt light and stretched thin as if she were disappearing, as if a light switch inside her was being shut off.

"No!" She heard her dad's voice somewhere above her, struggling, but she couldn't see him.

"I don't think so," boomed another voice, and a burst of bright purple light blinded her for just a moment. Babette.

Babette blasted the mob of ghosts off Lucely, giving her enough time to stand and begin capturing them again. Then Babette turned toward the fireflies and held out her hands, beckoning them to her. She seemed to be harnessing their light as they enveloped her. She looked like a giant flower made of lavender and white lights.

Simon now stood alongside Lucely, Syd, and Babette. To Lucely's surprise, he wasn't stopping her. He was backing them up like a bodyguard. The feel of his hand on her shoulder was reassuring; it was the only thing keeping her standing in place.

Mayor Anderson screamed, clearly annoyed at their resistance. "You witches are all the same! You just want to *take* what isn't yours and *hurt* the good people of this town."

"Leave the town out of this," Babette said. "This is between you and me, Braggs!"

Braggs? Lucely tore her eyes from the scene in front of her for just a moment and shot a look at Syd, who was staring back at her. So they *had* been right about Eliza Braggs.

Mayor Anderson laughed. His skin began to shift as if a wave were rippling beneath the surface. The spirit of Eliza Braggs now stood where Mayor Anderson had been just seconds before.

"I knew you'd try to meddle," Eliza Braggs said. "Knew you'd be just like the rest of your awful coven. They were always *such* an inconvenience—a group of troublesome women. Las Brujas Moradas have brought nothing but disease and disorder to St. Augustine ever since they arrived. I thought I'd wiped you all out the first time, but clearly I was wrong. I vowed to take my revenge against you for what that . . . Pilar girl did to my precious son. She poisoned him against me, and now I will make you lose what you love most."

The aura of light surrounding Babette pulsed brighter now, reminding Lucely of the invincibility power-up in *Super Mario Bros.*

"You can keep trying to cut us down, but our roots go deep," Babette said. "You will never succeed."

Eliza laughed at that. "Clever words won't save you now, witch. I will stop you once and for all, even if I have to use the souls of the townspeople to do it! Just like I used that little seer and your granddaughter. By midnight tonight—when the full moon is at its brightest—I will have raised the most powerful army St. Augustine has ever seen and *destroy* you all!"

With that, Eliza Braggs transformed once again, this time into a hideous, growling beast. She was ten feet tall and dripping with green ooze, long strands of scraggly hair hanging from her limbs like moss. Ghosts with black holes for eyes and mouths surrounded the creature, moaning and outstretching their hands toward Lucely, Syd, Babette, and Simon. The horde of ghosts shrouded the monster like the hood of a king cobra, keeping her deep in their shadow and away from the light. Babette's face lit up. The witch whipped her wrist in a circle, sending a needlelike point of light toward the demon and then back to Babette like a tiny boomerang.

Babette's attack weakened the monster, and beacons of light shone from the wounds her magic had made. The creature that was no longer Eliza shrieked.

"Hold on!" Babette commanded, then shot out toward the ghosts. Babette erupted, sending an enormous shock wave of light and energy exploding out from her body—her attack terrible and big.

Lucely couldn't tell if it was just her senses playing tricks on her, but the next moments seemed to unfold in slow motion and, aside from a faint ringing in her ears, absolute silence.

An ever-expanding dome of purple light froze any evil spirit it passed through in place. Eliza shifted back into her human form, her eyes full of fear, as the force trapped her.

For a moment, everything was still. Then with the sound of crashing thunder, the light collapsed back in on itself like a dying star, pulling the spirits in.

Lucely and Syd were launched backward by the force of the implosion, but Simon caught them and wrapped his arms around them both, shielding them from the flying debris. The ghosts and the beast were swept up into a giant tornado and went screaming out a window of the giant room, shattering it in their wake.

Silence fell on the room. When Lucely looked around, they were the only ones left standing.

"Don't worry about them. They'll be fine, so long as we can stop Eliza." Babette stumbled to her knees, weakened by the amount of magic she had just expended.

"Lucely, the paper. Where is it?" Babette asked hurriedly.

Lucely pulled the paper with the impossible riddle on it, the one from the catacombs, from her pocket.

"*A light to guide you through the night,*" she recited. "*Confront your fate before it's too late.*"

Lucely's eyes brightened as she thought of the beacons of light coming from the monster after Babette's attack.

"The lighthouse," Lucely said, remembering the marker on the spirit map that had disappeared.

Babette smiled knowingly. "We must get there before midnight."

"The lighthouse?" Simon asked, sounding more than a little out of breath.

"Las Brujas Moradas once convened at the old lighthouse. When they were banished, Eliza led a mob to burn it to the ground." Babette was back on her feet. "Our only hope of putting an end to what Eliza has set in motion rests with whatever residual magic we can draw from that place."

Lucely and Syd looked at each other. Babette looked at Simon. Simon looked confused.

"We'll explain everything in the car, Dad." Lucely tugged at his arm as they fled city hall. "We've got a city to save!"

CHAPTER TWENTY-ONE

"DID THAT MONSTER EAT Mayor Anderson?" Syd asked as they all piled into Babette's car.

"What just happened back there?" Simon slid into the back seat with Lucely and Syd.

"Meow." Chunk's voice was low and somehow laced with concern.

"Chunk!" Lucely and Syd said in unison.

"Seat belts!" Babette floored the gas, and they peeled out of the parking lot with a screech of tires and smoke, rain still coming down in sheets.

As they made it to the Bridge of Lions, which would take them to the lighthouse, a heavy fog settled around them, leaving almost nothing visible beyond it.

"So it *was* Eliza Braggs impersonating the mayor this whole time . . ." Lucely said.

"The same woman who accused Las Brujas Moradas of hexing her son?!" Syd added.

Babette nodded. "There was a lot of fear and superstition surrounding herbalists and healers in her time, and she wanted nothing more than to rid the town of their presence. However, a new generation of Las Brujas Moradas cropped up not long ago, reviving our magic and the commitment to protect the town. From the looks of it, I'm guessing that's what called her back here, to seek revenge."

"*Our?*" Syd, Lucely, and Simon all leaned forward in their seats.

Babette sighed. "Isn't it obvious? Honestly, I thought you girls would've figured it out sooner. I'm one of the witches of the Purple Coven. The younger generation anyway. Braggs knows that I have the power to stop her, that I can call on my coven, past and present, to stand against her."

"Is *anyone* gonna tell me what's going on?" Simon asked.

They tried their best to bring him up to speed, with Chunk supplying an occasional, insistent meow whenever she played a part in the story.

"How are we supposed to stop her army of evil spirits from destroying the whole town?" Simon asked.

"We go to the lighthouse—where the coven once met in secret—and recite the spell," Babette said, biting her lip.

"Except we only have the first half of the spell, remember?" Syd pointed out.

Babette scratched her head. "The spell was intended to help you, and you have to remember why you needed it in the first place to finish it. I think what's missing is an element that is personal."

Lucely's mind raced as she held her mason jar close, the fireflies pulsing brighter now than they had in weeks.

She remembered what Tía Milagros used to say when she was scared: *"Fear the living, mija, not the dead."* But now, it was the dead they were up against. Not Mayor Anderson, but a monster and her spirit army made of pure malice. And those spirits would be rising from their graves at midnight.

People walked around in costume, convinced the thick mist was a trick of the light or an illusion put on by the town for them. The streets were teaming with tourists, and though Lucely hoped the ghosts would be still, she knew better. Tonight, they would not be.

"Get to shelter, you big dummies!" Babette yelled through her window, but they only clapped and hooted. Some of them looked scared enough to turn back, and Lucely could only hope they were going inside somewhere safe.

When they reached the road leading to the lighthouse, the moon broke through the clouds overhead, illuminating the tower's black-and-white-striped exterior in the distance. Felled trees made navigating any farther by car impossible.

"Out!" Babette ordered. "We go the rest of the way on foot!"

Babette led them through the rain toward the lighthouse, which had always reminded Lucely of something out of *Beetlejuice*. Syd quickly explained how their Razzle-Dazzlers worked to Simon, who was now holding a spare Babette happened to have in her trunk.

"I'm glad you're here," Lucely said to him.

"Don't be too glad," he said. "Once this is all over, you're grounded till you're sixteen."

"Woof."

When they reached the entrance at the base of the tower, Babette made quick work of the locks and they all shuffled through the door, grateful—Chunk most of all—to have a refuge from the wind and rain.

Babette snapped her fingers, and a flame appeared in the palm of her hand. With a flick of her wrist, the flame began to float in midair, filling the room with a soft purple glow. "Look alive, gang. There could be any number of creatures in here waiting to attack us the moment we let our guard down."

They started up the spiral staircase leading to the top of the tower as Babette's light guided their way.

"How are we not to the top of this thing yet?" Lucely huffed. "I feel like we've been going in circles forever."

"Right?!" Syd was just as exhausted and confused. "Do you think it could be some sort of illusion, like when we were trying to reach the cathedral?"

Lucely and Syd reached the landing and collapsed on the floor while Simon and Babette unpacked their things.

"I am never getting up from this spot again," Syd groaned. "This is where I live now."

Chunk mewed angrily.

"Lucely, can you come here for a second? There's something I need to tell you before we do this." Babette's face was grim.

"Is everything okay?" Lucely asked, slightly panicked. Babette never acted nervous like this.

"The spell . . . Lucely, there are always consequences when it comes to magic. Sometimes sacrifices are required."

"What sacrifices?" Simon walked over and put one arm around Lucely's shoulder.

Babette sighed. "There's a chance that, if the spell is successful, your firefly spirits could disappear as well."

Lucely gasped, her hands reaching for the mason jar still hanging at her waist. No. She couldn't lose them. She was supposed to save them.

Lucely was completely overcome with rage and fear and sadness. This was all her fault.

She walked across the landing, closing her eyes and taking deep breaths to try to clear her head for just one moment. When she opened her eyes again, a thick black fog surrounded her. She could hear the muffled voices of her father, Syd, and Babette calling her name, but when she tried to shout back, it was like trying to yell underwater. She took a few steps forward, arms outstretched, but they were gone.

Something behind Lucely rustled. When she turned around, a shroud of darkness no longer surrounded her, and neither was she in the lighthouse. Instead, she was alone in the middle of a cemetery in the pouring rain. There were no more voices now—everything was deadly silent.

Something in Lucely's gut told her that this was just another trick, that Eliza was playing games with her to keep them from casting the counterspell before midnight. But the wind, the grass, the rain—it all felt so real. She looked around again and realized she recognized her surroundings: It was Huguenot Cemetery!

"I know how to get home from here," she whispered to herself, looking for a small piece of comfort.

Something whispered to her from the back of her mind, unbidden. But Lucely couldn't understand what it was trying to tell her. It was just beyond her reach.

Lucely thought of her father, of Mamá Teresa and the rest of her firefly ancestors, of Syd and Babette. They meant *everything* to her. She wouldn't let anything happen to her family, no matter what it cost.

As Lucely started to unravel the final piece of the spell, something flew past, knocking her to the ground. On instinct, she whipped out her Razzle-Dazzler and blasted an arc of rainbow light through the fog. Lucely immediately wished she hadn't.

The undead were everywhere. The fog was not just made of mist but of actual ghosts. They blanketed the entire sky; they were a wall of gray and black around her. Even the ground below her seemed translucent, a pool of ghosts dancing beneath her feet. Lucely screamed and began to trap them. There were more of them than she and the others had ever anticipated; not hundreds of ghosts, but *thousands*. Their attention was now fixed on Lucely.

The fireflies buzzed, and Lucely's hand hesitated over the mason jar. Hurting the fireflies was the last thing she wanted to do, but she wasn't sure she could do this alone.

She needed to get back to her family, back to the lighthouse. A gap opened in the fog and a team of ghosts burst through. A group of people in pointy hats. *Witches*, Lucely thought. And the people from her dad's historic paintings, Enriquillo and the Mirabal sisters . . . and another man Lucely recognized. It was Judge John Stickney—the ghost who was missing his teeth. They rushed forward and for a moment Lucely held up her Razzle-Dazzler instinctively, but instead of attacking her, they dove for the ghosts keeping her trapped.

"Help the girlie get through!" Judge John yelled as he led the attack. The witches moved in tandem, magic wands up in one hand, holding their large skirts up with the other. They blasted group after group of ghosts, trying to create an opening big enough for Lucely to get through. Her heart beat so hard she could hear it pounding in her ears. The sky beyond the wall of ghosts turned darker as they fought their way out, as if all the lights in the world were being turned off at once.

But the path was still not big enough for Lucely to get through. She needed more help and looked down to her fireflies as they flashed their lights trying to get her attention. She knew they wanted to help, and she knew she had to let them if she had any hope of escaping.

"Please be safe," she whispered into the fog, her eyes closed for just a moment, and opened the latch on her jar.

Tiny lights erupted from the mason jar, and where there was a small path created by her Razzle-Dazzler and the friendly ghosts before, there was now a massive tunnel of brilliant light. The ghosts pushed on all sides of the tunnel, trying to break through, but her fireflies created a golden net, keeping them back. Lucely ran, straight through the tunnel without looking back. She had to get back to her family quickly, and nothing else mattered in that moment. Because she had the final piece of the spell.

CHAPTER TWENTY-TWO

LUCELY AWOKE WITH A START, gasping for air as if she had nearly drowned. The room around her slowly came into focus. She was back at the lighthouse, lying on the floor, with Babette, Syd, and her dad standing over her.

Babette produced one of the small strawberry candies she always seemed to have in her pockets and offered it to Lucely. "Here, this'll help."

"Luce! You're not dead!" Syd squealed, nearly tackle-hugging her.

"Goonies . . . never say . . . die," Lucely groaned from the hug, her body still stiff from lying on the concrete floor for who knows how long. But she didn't pull away either.

Simon reached over and squeezed her shoulder. "I'm glad you're okay, kiddo. But I knew you would be. You're always so strong, stronger than I could ever be."

"That's not true. Where do you think I get it from?" Lucely smiled at Simon.

"Are we going to hug one another all night or get down to business?" Babette asked despite the clear look of relief on her face. "What did you see?"

"Um . . ." Lucely began. "Well, one moment I was standing here, and the next I was alone in a cemetery—the Huguenot—when I was attacked by thousands of spirits. Some part of me knew it was a vision, but it felt so real."

"And did you get what you needed?"

She nodded, and Babette gave her the scroll of paper and a pen.

"Write it down, quickly, before you forget. You and Syd will need to recite it no matter what happens. I've already prepared the space."

Lucely wasn't sure how, but Babette must've known the spell would come to her during the vision.

Dozens of lit candles flickered around the red viewing platform, their light weaving with the fireflies' light as they flew in and out of the room.

Babette pointed at the spirit storm building on the sea in the light of the moon.

"I need your toughest firefly, Lucely. The scariest of them all."

Lucely nearly smiled, and then in unison with Syd and her father said, "Tía Milagros."

Lucely tapped on her mason jar and called for her tía, and moments later, she emerged.

"What do we do?" Tía Milagros's voice arrived before her human form did, but soon she was standing next to Babette, chancla in hand.

"We use these." Babette flourished her cape to reveal tiny mirrors along its edges. "And the lenses there." She pointed at the giant rotating lenses within the lighthouse enclosure.

"Now we just need the help of Las Brujas—"

"Moradas," Tía Milagros said. "I know those stories well."

"As a member of the coven, I can invoke their spirits here tonight. More than their spirits, their energy, their power." Babette turned to Tía Milagros and smiled. "Can you get me up to the lens? Lucely and Syd, when you see a light flare from us, just as the light from this beacon comes around for the third time, you begin the spell. Simon, you and Chunk cover the girls. Got it?"

They all nodded.

"Let's go," Babette said.

Tía Milagros nodded and then became a bright white light, enveloping Babette and taking her out into the storm.

The beam from the lighthouse came around, illuminating the spirit storm. It was a shapeless form, and as it came closer, Lucely saw that it was made of a disgusting gray slimy substance. It groaned with what sounded like the voices of hundreds of lost souls.

With her father, Syd, and Chunk by her side, Lucely watched as Babette opened her cape and revealed a magic wand. Lucely was anxious but on high alert, waiting for the signal for her to recite the spell with Syd.

The spirit storm seemed to notice Babette standing at attention on the topmost platform of the lighthouse now and grew in all different directions, like a ten-thousand-headed monster. It roared at Babette and gained speed as it charged toward them. Babette shot a bolt of purple light from her wand, briefly stunning the spirit storm.

Babette raised her arms and began to intone a spell, her voice booming in the night sky so loudly that Lucely wouldn't have been surprised if all of Florida could hear her. Her cape was spread out on both sides and seemed to go on for miles. The tiny mirrors glittered in the moonlight.

"Las Brujas Moradas, hear us tonight.

No longer in hiding, no longer in fright.

Las Brujas Moradas, come to our call.

No longer afraid, to tumble and fall.

Las Brujas, Las Brujas, answer our plea.

Come to us now, from land and from sea.
Take this demon away, tonight,
Las Brujas Moradas.
Take this demon from sight!"

Twinkling purple stars began to shower down all around them. Brilliant and bright, they fell like snow before settling into their human forms on the viewing platform. The brujas surrounded Babette as she moved to stand next to the massive lens. Light pulsed from their hands as they transmitted their energy to Babette.

When the light from the beacon came around again, Babette bellowed, "Now!"

"It's now or never, Syd," Lucely said.

Syd nodded, tears forming in her eyes. They were both shaking, perhaps from the wind or fear, or probably both. But Lucely fixed Syd with a determined look and squeezed her hands. *We can do this*, she tried to tell her. *We're gonna do it together.*

Lucely took a deep breath and began.

"A sprinkle of sun,
A shimmer of light,
Turn back the darkness,
Turn back the fright . . ."

A swarm of spirits closed in on them, but Simon fought them back with a Razzle-Dazzler in each hand, shooting as if he'd been doing this his whole life. Chunk hissed and swatted at any ghost that got too close, occasionally growing to her mega-Chunk size and roaring in their faces.

Lucely took a jagged deep breath, her hands shaking so hard she could barely keep hold of Syd.

"We've got this," Syd yelled over the howling wind. "I believe in you, Lucely!"

"MEOW," added Chunk.

Lucely felt the warmth of the fireflies around her, as if they were saying, "We believe in you too!"

She closed her eyes and finished the spell from the heart.

"I call on the power
Of my ancestor's ghosts
And speak three names, I love most . . .
Simon Luna, Teresa Luna, and Syd Faires!"

Light shot out from Syd's and Lucely's clasped hands straight toward Babette and Las Brujas. Magnified by the lighthouse's lens, an explosion of purple and white lit up the night sky. The bright lights reflected off Babette's cape and surged—bigger and bigger—until finally the dazzling blaze of purple-and-white light seemed to engulf the entire ocean. Everything was shaking, and the lighthouse seemed moments from collapsing around them.

A massive, swirling gateway formed in the sky above the lighthouse, dragging the spirit storm across its threshold as if Tía Milagros were vacuuming them all up.

The ghosts wailed as they flew into the void and a final rush of fog overtook them, making a sound like a roller coaster rumbling overhead. The sky above the lighthouse roared shut, leaving nothing but silence and the light of the fireflies, blinking out.

CHAPTER TWENTY-THREE
TWO DAYS LATER

WHEN LUCELY OPENED HER EYES, she saw her father sitting in the chair next to her bed, a huge, goofy smile on his face.

"Welcome back to the land of the living, kiddo." Simon held out a bowl of cold farina.

"You put it in the fridge," she croaked. "That's my favorite."

"Yes, I could never forget." Her dad smiled proudly. "You are my child, after all."

Cold farina was Lucely's favorite thing to eat for breakfast back when her mother was around, but her dad had stopped making anything Lucely's mom used to make because it hurt him too much. Now there was no hurt in his face. There was only love.

Lucely's eyes flew open, as she suddenly remembered everything. "Did it work?" Is everyone okay? The fireflies? Mamá?"

Lucely's heart nearly stopped waiting for her father to answer.

"I . . . think they're okay. You know I can't see them the way you can, but they're all in place, all flying and shining."

She would have to check on them, but they had to be okay. They just had to be.

"And it did work, Luce. You girls saved the town from a vengeful mega-ghost with an army of nasty spirits. Not to mention you and Syd are local heroes now." Simon held up a newspaper for her to see. "The *Gazette* delivered a special issue to every house in St. Augustine yesterday morning. You two made the front page!"

LOCAL BEST FRIENDS SAVE ST. AUGUSTINE

At just twelve years old, best friends Lucely Luna, daughter of Simon Luna, owner and operator of the remarkably charming Luna Ghost Tour, and Syd Faires, granddaughter of Babette's Baubles proprietor Babette Faires, have already made their mark on St. Augustine. When a record-breaking storm made landfall on Sunday night, Lucely and Syd found themselves at a crossroads.

"Well, we were biking over to city hall for the Halloween Festival when we noticed that the lighthouse's beacon wasn't lit, which was odd," Syd Faires explained. "So we decided to check it out for ourselves." According to her firsthand account, by the time the girls reached the lighthouse, the sky had opened up and rain was coming down in torrents. Seeking shelter inside, they discovered that the lighthouse's power grid had been completely shut off. "Now, I'm no expert when it comes to electrical work, but when I see a massive switch that says 'off' and 'on,' I can handle it myself," Faires said. Once the lighthouse's power grid was back online, the emergency alert sensors came alive. Now alight, the beacon could fulfill its purpose: guiding travelers, both on land and at sea, out of harm's way. The quick and decisive action of these two girls may just have saved lives.

As the sun rose on a new day, the brute strength of the storm was on full display. Rebuilding will take years, but if we've learned anything from our past, it's that those who gather around a unifying cause and help one another create a stronger and more resilient community, prepared to weather any storm that dares to try to divide them.

"I don't understand," Lucely said. "None of that is true. Everyone at city hall saw what happened that night."

"Are you sure about that, Luce?" Simon raised an eyebrow. "What's the name of the newspaper again?"

She inspected the front page. At the top, in bold, gothic type, were the words the *Babette Gazette*. Lucely looked confused. "Babette wrote this?!"

"Pretty good, right?" Babette glided into the room trailed by Syd. "I'm glad you've finally woken up. You two left quite a mess in my library."

"I think I'm feeling kind of sleepy now, actually," said Syd, and Lucely laughed.

Chunk tried to jump onto Lucely's bed and failed, so Syd hefted her up, setting her in Lucely's lap.

"I'm glad you're okay, Syd," Lucely said.

"Me?! You're the one who's been knocked out. My parents even came by to play some music to help you heal, or something hippie-ish. You slept through my dad's saxaphone *and* my mom's drums. Think about that."

The girls laughed, and Lucely quirked an eyebrow.

"What about the attack at city hall? The mayor turning into an evil spirit and wreaking havoc all over town? Everyone at the Halloween Festival saw what really happened."

"People are all too willing to believe an easy lie in place of a complicated truth." Babette flourished her hand as she spoke. "Anyone with, say, a talent for the craft of deception can bend the truth just enough to turn one's memory of events into something more . . . palatable for the general public."

Syd rolled her eyes. "What Babette is *trying* to say is that, once everyone in town had recovered from her magic shock wave–thingy that banished the evil spirits at City Hall and wiped their memory, she enchanted these newspapers so that anyone who read them would remember my grandma's creative-writing version of history."

Lucely scrunched her face. "Kind of like that red flashy thing they use in *Men in Black*?"

"'Woman in Purple' doesn't quite have the same ring to it though," Simon said, laughing.

"Whoa, that's . . . so cool!" It was all starting to click into place for Lucely.

Simon's face softened. "You've missed a lot in the past two days, Luce."

"They found the real Mayor Anderson locked in the basement of city hall rambling on about how Eliza Braggs had ghost-napped him," Syd cut in. "Though he didn't know she was a ghost at the time."

"I had to whip up a little something special just for him." Babette winked at Lucely.

"Speaking of which, why didn't Syd sleep for two days?" Lucely sat up and the room spun.

"The magic took a lot out of you," Babette explained. "And as it turns out . . ."

"I'm a witch!" Syd pounced onto the bed, and even though it made the room spin again, Lucely laughed.

"Witch *in training*," Babette corrected. "You've got a lot to learn before you can call yourself a true witch."

Lucely squealed with excitement at Syd's news, wrapping her in a hug. "I can't believe it. My best friend is a *witch*!"

"I know! I can't wait to hex our classmates," Syd said.

"Sydney . . ." Babette's voice was low.

"I'm kidding!" Syd said. "I'm not kidding," she whispered into Lucely's ear.

Lucely laughed and sank into Syd's arms. "Thanks for believing in me, Syd. And for sticking by my side throughout all this. I couldn't have done it without you."

Syd smiled. "That's what I'm here for. Cracking jokes and kicking ghost butt and being charming. I could go on."

Lucely and Syd broke into a fit of giggles.

The phone in the hallway rang, waking a grumpy Chunk from her nap.

"I'll get it," Simon said, stepping out of the room. "Luna Ghost Tour . . . no, sorry. We're all booked through Halloween.

Yes, of next year, I'm so sorry! I will keep your name on the waiting list in case of a cancellation. Yes, of course. Thank you!"

Lucely felt like her eyes might pop out of her head. "Halloween of *next year*?"

"That's right," Simon said. "With all the media attention around you and Syd—thanks to Babette's article—we've been flooded with calls and bookings for the past two days."

"Does that mean that we don't have to move?" Lucely asked hopefully.

"The Lunas are officially here to stay! And we're going to help St. Augustine get back on its feet. After the destruction caused by Eliza Braggs and her spirit storm, the town needs us here more than ever."

Lucely beamed at her dad, happy that some more good had come of all this.

"Have you made her the tea?" Babette asked Simon as she put one hand on Lucely's forehead.

"Oh, not yet. I'll go do that now. I'll be right back, kid," Simon said as he and Babette walked out, Babette giving him instructions the entire way.

"Lucely, can I ask you something sorta weird?" Syd asked.

"When have you ever asked permission for that?" Lucely joked before seeing that Syd was being serious.

"Way harsh, but fair. I was just wondering . . ." Syd tugged at her sleeve. "When you were reciting the last part of the spell, why did you say my name and not your mother's?"

Lucely chewed her lip. "When I blacked out, ghosts helped me escape in my vision, and I saw the spirits of all the historical figures my dad has hanging up around our house. They reminded me of home, and when I thought of home . . . I thought of you. I could just feel the final piece of the spell had to come from my heart. I spent a lot of time thinking about how much I missed my mom, how much I wished I had my family back together again. But then I realized that I already have a family." She smiled at Syd. "My dad and you and Babette and the fireflies. Even all the Goonies cats."

"Can you even imagine what that family portrait would look like?" They both laughed at this.

Chunk rolled onto her back next to Lucely. "Meow," she agreed.

"Maybe family is more than who you're related to," Lucely said. "It's also the people you find and love along the way."

"I had no idea you were so deep, Lucely!" Syd teased.

Lucely rubbed Chunk's belly and shrugged playfully. "The deepest. I'm, like, a poet or something."

"I'm really glad you're not moving away," Syd said, squeezing her again.

Lucely sank back into her bed, smiling. "Me too, Syd."

Just then, a warm breeze swept through Lucely's open window, and the room began to fill with a light so bright that Lucely and Syd had to pull the blanket up to shield their eyes. After a few moments, Lucely dared to peek, squinting her eyes as they adjusted to the dimming glow that now surrounded her.

Macarena and Manny, Tía Milagros and Tía Rosario, Tío Celestino, Benny and Yesenia—everyone in her spirit family was there, standing around her bed, smiling.

"You're all okay." She beamed. "I was worried that I'd lost you forever."

Tía Milagros reached out and took Lucely's hand. "Our place is here. With you."

Macarena jumped onto the bed and hugged Lucely so tightly she could barely breathe.

Her spirit family parted to let through another shimmering light. As it came closer and closer, the light began to take shape. The woman before her smiled—a million wrinkles lining her face and the brown liver spots on her hands peeking out from her flowery sleeves.

As she came closer, Lucely smiled, her face wet with tears.

"Mamá," she choked out.

Mamá Teresa sat on the bed, and Lucely threw herself into her abuela's arms.

"No pasa nada, mi niña," Mamá said as she smoothed Lucely's frizzed hair and began singing softly to her.

"Everything is okay," Lucely said, smiling back at Mamá, and she knew she was home.

ACKNOWLEDGMENTS

First, I want to thank God for listening to my prayers sometimes and letting me learn the hard way other times. It was needed.

To my parents, Anazaria and Pablo, for always supporting me, telling me I can do anything I put my mind to, and showing me that life isn't perfect or easy. To my sisters: Nina, you are always there for me when I need you. Thank you for the advice, the tough love, the annoying wake-up calls when we shared a room. I love you so much! Jeanny, thank you for showing me what strength looks like. I don't know how you do it, but your smile and your perseverance inspire me. I'm proud you're my big sister, even if you're really annoying sometimes too.

David, thank you for believing in my writing before I did. We've grown up together, and we've been through *it all*. I wouldn't trade the years of challenges, of being Pancho's parents, of loving you for anything. Thanks for always being there and always spoiling me with cookies. None of the things I've accomplished would be as fun without you to scream about them with. Thanks for brainstorming with me, for helping me figure out plot holes, for putting up with my emotions when I'm on deadline. We make the best team, and I love you more than you know. Please translate this for Pancho, preferably in the form of string cheese. ☺ I love you bud. Let's make a fort now, please!

To my nieces and nephews (I'm taking a deep breath because there a lot of you. Related: good job, sisters) in age order: Gigi, aka Comeongi, I am so happy at how you're growing up. So smart and so tall and so kind and patient. I'm excited for my future free teeth cleanings. I love you so, so much. The foot thing was Joshua's fault.

To Joshua, man where do I start, Joshie-poo? You've been one of my best pals since you were born. Thank you for helping me select outfits at Charlotte Russe when you were two, for finishing *Kingdom Hearts* with me, for standing there motionless and silent while I recorded music—rofl (I'm still sorry for that), and for sending me memes when I'm sad. I love you, and I'm so proud of you. Please be sure to budget a bougie apartment for me when you graduate MIT. ☺ Thanks for being so super excited for

Ghost Squad; your enthusiasm for it gave me confidence. #ForeverYachtAccess

Evan, I love how caring and kind you've always been, even when you were chasing Gigi with the chair that one time. You're so incredibly talented, and I can't listen to you sing without crying. Thank you for being one of my first-ever beta readers and for having so much enthusiasm for my world and my writing. I'll never forget it.

To Sam: You're one of the best kids on this planet. So funny, so smart, so loving. Thanks for letting me read chapters of my writing to you, for reading ghost books with me during sleepovers, for making me laugh, and for making me proud. You're the kind of kid I wrote this book for, and I won't lie, a lot of Syd's snarky lines and jokes were written with you in mind, lol. Thanks for inspiring me.

Maia, my February buddy. You're such an amazing writer, and I love how voracious a reader you are. Thanks for giving me feedback on my chapters and for almost making me name this book *Fireflies of Passion*.

To L, the best bro-in-law I could ever ask for! Can't wait to raise my champagne glass like a '90s video with you at the launch party. You're the best. <3

Pedro, thanks for all your support throughout the years!

To my INCREDIBLE agent, Suzie Townsend: I'm really happy you're in my corner. Thank you for believing in me and for making me a better writer. I've learned so much from you, and I appreciate you so, so much. I hope to keep selling books so you can play the dragon app again one day.

To everyone at New Leaf and especially Dani Segelbaum, Cassandra Baim, and Meredith Barnes: You are all my heroes, and I can't believe I get to work with such amazing people.

To everyone at Scholastic: my editor, Jeffrey West; Lizette Serrano; David Levithan; and all the sales, marketing, and publicity people—I couldn't ask for a better team to champion my book. Thank you for everything you've done for me and for *Ghost Squad*.

To my very first critique partners and beta readers— Michael Mammay and Andrea Contos: I would not be here without your help. Mike, thanks for telling me some hard truths about my writing and getting me on the path to publication. You're one of my favorite people on this planet. Andrea, thanks for being one of my closest friends and most trusted confidants, for making our own private group chat to get away from the weirdos, for supporting me through querying and the query welcome-back center, for all the laughs, for the KH tweets, and for the support during grief and offers and setbacks. I love you!

To Kat and Beth: What in the world would I do without our group chat? Kat, I never imagined I'd make one of my best friends in life as an old woman, but here we are. Thanks for being there for me always, for celebrating with me, and for listening to me. I'm lucky to have you in my life and happy to share this journey with you. Beth, thank you for creating DVPIT, for helping to change my life, and for being one of the fiercest, funniest friends I've ever had. #BODforever #KatSubtweet

To Patrice Caldwell—*Ghost Squad* would not have happened without you. Thank you for believing in me when nobody else in publishing did. I will never forget your support and your encouragement.

To Leigh Bardugo for your priceless advice and your patience with my annoying emails. You taught me how to be both legendary and humble just by being you.

To Peter Lopez for being my number one stan, my reality show shishter, my support, and my nonstop texting buddy. Thank you for reading *Ghost Squad*, for reading ALL my books, and for helping me without hesitation every time. Love you so much, PERIOD! Can't wait to see your books on shelves very soon.

To the *Write or Die* podcast community: Thank you for supporting me always. I'm so grateful for all our listeners.

To the many, many friends, authors, readers, and teachers who've supported me on my path to publication: Chris & Julie Bujarski, Stephanie Ford, Jackie Senno, Jessica & Chris

Sevigny, Julie C. Dao, the Writing Cult, Connie and Lucas, Josie, Katie Bailey, Ozma, Pete Forester, Ryan La Sala, Eric Smith, Zoraida C., Suzanne Samin, Samira Ahmed, Tiffany Jackson, Isabel Sterling, Sierra Elmore, Laura Sebastian, Adam Silvera, Cristina Arreola, and every last person online and everywhere who's supported me.

To anyone I left out: I'm sorry, but please know you're in my heart and that I am very sleepy all the time.

Last but not least, thank you to cheese. I would not have survived writing this or any book, without you.

ABOUT THE AUTHOR

Photo by Claribel A. Ortega

Claribel A. Ortega is a former reporter who writes middle-grade and young adult fantasy inspired by her Dominican heritage. When she's not busy turning her obsession with eighties pop culture, magic, and video games into books, she's traveling the world for her day job in marketing and making GIFs for her small graphic design business, GIFGRRL. You can find her on Twitter at @Claribel_Ortega and on her website at claribelortega.com.